GOOD MORNING, SIR GEORGE

Ten Tales of the Tinier Type

from

Donald Yule

With

Marion Pitman

making up the XI

CONTENTS

Ten Tales of the Tinier Type

And making up the XI

BY WAY OF INTRODUCTION ...

... and explanation

"Sweet are the uses of adversity". Thus muses Shakespeare's Duke Senior in *As You Like It* [Act 2 Sc.1] when exiled in the Forest of Arden. In the Spring of 2020, of horrible recent memory, I, in common with many, became briefly exiled from the company of others. This collection of whimsies is the product of that time.

The theme: *"Good morning Sir George"*, which percolates these pieces, arises from a remark I made once upon a day in the Pavilion at Lord's Cricket Ground to my friend Marion Pitman: *"One thing about this place that I like, is that you are always likely to see someone called 'Sir George'!"* Recollection of this aside, prompted me enter entirely new ground and construct ten [very] short stories, all of which would share the same starting and closing words but would be set in different times, different places and with different - but perhaps in some ways similar -persons called "Sir George". This little pamphlet is the result of those efforts.

Having made the remark to Marion, an acclaimed short story writer, I felt I should invite her to contribute and I am obliged to her for lending her expertise in Chapter 11. But this is not just a vanity exercise, for the royalties from this work will all go to the RNLI. I have drawn upon material assembled from many sources which I duly acknowledge in a postscript to each Tale. I hope that this little collection of "What possibly might have been" tales might raise a smile as you while away a rainy afternoon.

DONALD YULE

St Leonard's On Sea, E. Sussex   donyule@the-pres.org.uk

OCTOBER 1959

"Good morning, Sir George."

The words came chorused from the two young people whom Sir George, from his corner nook in Kardomah's Coffee House in central Manchester, had noticed before and were now standing alongside the table where, as was his wont, he had been the solitary occupant for some twenty minutes.

"Sorry to interrupt but we would like to join you". The words were from the man. The woman with him was clearly not going to take "No" as an answer as she sat down opposite Sir George in a fashion which indicated a clear intent. Her companion joined her and so the two confronted the somewhat startled Sir George across the table. *"Well at least I'm going to find out who these people are"* he thought.

He had seen the couple often on his regular early morning visits to this oasis in the busy heart of Manchester's commercial and administrative district. A business rather than a romantic attachment had been his verdict for never was any sign of affection nor any show of a wedding ring. Dressed in the usual attire of office workers, they were Boss and Secretary possibly, though the young woman had a positive air about her. They had been careful to keep their voices low so he had never picked up the subject of their often-argumentative conversations. He had concluded they were northerners, which was welcome to a man who had an aversion for the southern English in general and Londoners in particular. He had picked up a Manchester accent in the man and having heard the woman say "Och" on an occasion, placed her as Scottish.

"You seem to know who I am" he began. "But I do not know who you are. If you are going to sit here, then I would very much like to know who I'm talking to."

"Please don't be alarmed, Sir George. We are in the Police - but we've just come off duty. I'm Detective Sergeant Flashman and this is WPC Brown. It was her idea we talk to you."

"I have to say I've noticed you before and wondered who you were. How did you know me?"

"We would be failing in our duty to the public if we were not to recognise Manchester's leading citizens" was DS Flashman's reply, to which the WPC added: "The local papers all have you as this City's leading businessman - and you are always backing Manchester - what did the *Evening News* say last week? - 'a Mancunian in the greatest tradition of our commercial giants' and 'Our proudest Mancunian'".

Sir George was not unaccustomed to flattery but he WAS proud of his city and his family's part in its rise to prominence- the mines, the mills, that first railway from the port of Liverpool and then - closer to his own time - especially the Ship Canal and the docks. On the odd occasions he was sailing down the canal, a passenger on one of his company's vessels, he would ponder on the fact that the huge embankments built to carry the diverted railway lines high over the waterway had been the biggest ever earthworks carried out in Britain. He would always smile at thought of the slender overbridge near Warrington having been erected so as the local Banking magnate could reach his Head Office without let or hindrance .

He was smiling now as he spotted a juxtaposition of surnames: "Flashman and Brown, eh?" he remarked.

"You can see our Warrant Cards if you like" said the Detective Sergeant, rather annoyed at this seeming disbelief of identity.

"No need! Not at all! It was just the Rugby School connection I thought rather a coincidence."

"Rugby School?" queried DS Flashman. "I'm from Crumpsall. Our family name was Fleischman until the First World War and I know nowt about Rugby!"

"And I'm a Broon frae Balfron" expostulated his colleague. "I was at school in Stirling and then I was a student in Glasgow!"

"My joke – my apologies" said Sir George realising that neither of his younger companions had recognised the coincidence.

"Accepted" said the Detective Sergeant, still rather puzzled.

"To get back to the subject" said his colleague, keen to get to the point. "Sir George, you are very proud of this city?"

"Yes I am proud. But I'm also very worried. We are a great inland port – we trade directly with the likes of Toronto in Canada and Detroit in the USA but it's all coming to an end. Ships are getting bigger and bigger and anything much longer than five hundred foot won't fit into our locks."

"Oh" said WPC Brown. "I hadn't realised that!"

"Take it from me lass" continued Sir George who had now got into an accustomed full flow.

"I know that if people elsewhere think of Manchester", he continued. "They think of football first and then football second - then possibly cricket rained off at Old Trafford. Ask them to think a bit deeper and they'll mention the Ship Canal but without realising we have been one of the world's great inland ports. But it's all going to go and folk don't seem to recognise that. All this living in the past – it's not like us – it won't do!" Sir George thumped the table and spoons rattled in the crockery. One or two customers turned their heads in interest but Sir George went on.

"This city – this whole area- has to change. Communications made this city great – so that is where we must go – we must develop Ringway Airport - it has half a million passengers a year already, you know -we will need these new motorways – that Stretford Eccles Bypass is just the start – and why did we do away with the trams? - they could link with the railways – and we need to connect London Road Station to Victoria and Central Station isn't very central. There is lots to do - I said lots to do - if we are to keep our city as one of the world's great trading cities. Eh - I'm sorry – I'm going on - but if they don't wake up round here, then London'll take it all –I said - take it all!"

"You want to keep Manchester at the centre of things, then" said the Detective Sergeant from Crumpsall, aware of interest at neighbouring tables and rather hoping he could quieten things.
"Anything that will make people say: 'That's good - that's from Manchester'" Sir George replied, quietly but still with some force.
The Sergeant glanced at his colleague.
"We might have found something which will turn people's eyes our way", he said quietly and cautiously.
"How's that then?" Sir George had resumed his quieter mode.
"There's a side of life in this city, away from all these important offices and wonderful buildings, that you may not know about, Sir George", said the policeman, still warily.
"I know my city -warts and all young man. Manchester is as Manchester does."
"Good. Well -er- WPC Brown and I have to keep an eye on that side of things and in the course of our duties we've had regular contact with a young man called Tony. You tell him

Brownie. It's you that thinks he needs saving; I just try to uphold the law."

Sir George began to have an inkling of why the conversations he had witnessed might have been so argumentative but the Scots lass now had the floor.

"This Tony - he's sort of involved in television - has got an idea for a TV series based on round here. It's about the people in a street. There's a corner shop at one end and a pub at the other."

"Well that would be true to life!" Sir George was startled.

"He's got recognisable characters - big old bossy lady, a loose woman, a pub landlady who thinks she's above the rest – a tough guy builder and ..."

" .. and old biddys drinking stout in the snug?" asked Sir George, latching on to the idea - to the delight of the WPC.

" Well he's got a group of gossips – yes. It IS real - he does mean it and he's written bits too. He gave me a copy sheet of a bit he'd done, just to prove it."

She reached inside her shoulder bag and produced a folded flimsy sheet – clearly the carbon copy from a typescript. Sir George switched to his reading glasses and perused the paper.

"If that's the title 'Florizel Street' – then, that won't do -won't do at all – far too fancy and southern!"

"Och! That could be changed!"

"Well young lady why have you two brought this to me?

Flashman had to make a point: "Her idea, not mine Sir George. Our job's to uphold the Law as it is -- not act as social reformers"

"Our city's had its fair share of social reformers," admonished the older man. " What is it you want me to do?"

"We know that you know the big boss at Granada" said the DS.

"How do you know that?"

"We're detectives – or at least I am."

"You're right of course. It's me that's taught him how to be a true Northerner. And a champion job he's made of those new television studios – that's showed the southerners something!"

"He listens to you then?" queried the WPC.

"Definitely – I taught him about rain and Rugby League, Blackpool holidays and Bury black pudding."

DS Flashman was about to remark that all those did not exactly reflect Sir George's social background but thought better of it.

Brown had got exactly to where she had hoped to be and so pressed home her point.

"Then he would listen if he thought you had come across a good northern idea for a series?"

"Of course," he stated firmly. "But why does it have to be me?"

"Because Tony has tried everywhere. He spoke to the BBC - they thought it was a boring idea. People here don't take him seriously."

"We don't want the BBC doing something like this. They'd do it in London with southerners imitating accents - they haven't got a clue - can't tell Lancashire from Yorkshire. No if we're going to have a bit of real northern life - it has to be done here - with local actors."

"I have to say this –" admitted the DS. "Brownie read me a bit of that paper - he's got Manchester - well Salford really – off to a tee."

The Scots policewoman adopted her most pleading tone and looked straight into Sir George's eyes. "When you next

see the Big Boss, can you please show him that piece of paper – can you get him to ask   one of his producers to contact Tony – I wrote his address and a telephone number at the bottom there – it's one we've come to know quite well!"
"I can hardly say no, can I? It might be seen as obstructing the police! Don't worry lass – I'll do just that - though that title won't do. I'll have to go now but this has been the most remarkable meeting."
"And we're off now too. It's the end of a long night," said Flashman.
"But perhaps the start of a new story" chimed in Brown.
Sir George rose to his feet: "Who knows? If the idea flops then I can say because it's based on Salford and not really Manchester."

Minutes later walking out into a rainy Mosley Street, Sir George suddenly found his mood lightened. He would indeed seek out Bernstein at the earliest opportunity and nudge him in the direction of the new concept. Irrespective of what the rest of the day had to throw at him, he could count himself as having had a **GOOD MORNING**.

AUTHOR'S POSTSCRIPT

Written in affectionate memory of Kardomah's Coffee Houses and the cargo liners from Manchester that used to pass along the Ship Canal when the author was a lad in Warrington. Homage also to the "Soap of Soaps" – Tony Warren's creation of *Coronation Street* and with fond memories of Ena Sharples, Elsie Tanner, Annie Walker, Len Fairclough etc – colourful characters on a black and white screen.

Apologies to my southern English friends!

JUNE 1940

"Good morning, Sir George."

With some reluctance, Sir George Welland arose slowly from his chair as his secretary showed in his visitor. He had been seated at his old- fashioned desk in his office, high in the Air Ministry building in London's Aldwych, which he had occupied since being plucked from his comfortable civilian existence in September 1939. Now, in this last week of June 1940, those days of designing the next generation of airliners seemed so far off.

Now he was faced with the awesome responsibility of making recommendations upon which the very future of Britain and its Empire might depend. His immediate worry was the future of the RAF's fighter aircraft. He was more than happy with decisions taken well before he had any input. The Spitfire and the Hurricane looked winners - especially when converted to 100-octane fuel - but there was the problem of sheer numbers.

Despite what Beaverbrook [whom Sir George saw as a Canadian money-grabbing upstart], was telling him- or rather declaiming at him – Sir George agreed with the consensus opinion that the RAF would have to buy fighters from abroad, and abroad now meant the USA. However, he had been strongly against the Purchasing Commission's decision to ask the North American Aircraft Co. to produce the Curtiss P40 Warhawk fighter, an admirable aircraft in its way but, in his opinion, lacking the high altitude capability that the RAF would need for what Churchill had suggested would be a "Battle of Britain". So he had been secretly rather pleased when, back in the Spring, the US constructors demurred over producing someone else's old design and instead suggested their own more modern idea. Sir George liked the look of that though he wondered whether the suggested engine would be sufficient - perhaps that could be remedied later when there were enough of the splendid Rolls Royce Merlins available. But all these matters lay in the realm of piston engined, propeller driven aircraft, a world in which he felt familiar. What was troubling him now was the prospect of jet propulsion.

The matter had been raised in the previous month when he had met newly appointed Secretary of State for Air: The Right Honourable Sir Archibald Sinclair Bt. KT CMG, MP for Caithness and Sutherland and Leader of the Liberal party. Although he thought the man's politics too wishy-washy, Sir George liked the new man much more than either of his predecessors. Consequently, he was prepared to listen and took on board the fact that Britain should now be thinking seriously about accelerating the development of jet-propelled aircraft. But that was a world of which he had only the sketchiest knowledge and so had been immersing himself in all the latest about rockets, pulsejets, turbojets. He had familiarised himself with the work of a chap called Whittle of the Power Jets company with their new engine and how Gloster Aircraft were to build an aircraft which would test it.. They had an Air Ministry Specification to work to – but how was that proceeding? And, of course, what were the Germans up to.

He had known for some time there must be a limit to the performance of propeller-driven aircraft but he was now struggling to assimilate the welter of data now before him. Thus the arrival of the worried -looking young man, with the American accent and continental cut of clothes, who had greeted him was in some ways an unwelcome interruption, forced on him by a strange phone call from a "Mr Jermyn" the previous day.

On his secretary putting him though he heard a typically upper-class English educated voice:
"Sir George, for the purposes of this call and any other contact, my name is Mr. Jermyn and I am with the Security Service. Now - I know exactly how important your work is in developing this country's military aircraft but we have a problem with which, I feel you may be able to help us."
Sir George found himself muttering a rather puzzled assent.
"Thank you. Trouble is -we have a young American chappie who's suddenly wandered in from Sweden having been in Germany for some years and getting to know a lot of important people in their aircraft industry. Our man in Sweden tipped us off but we're not sure what to make of him. Reminds me rather of that writer chap – Ransome - who knew all the top Bolshies. It was years before we could figure him out."
This allusion puzzled Sir George but he said nothing.
" Well this chappie – he's called Eugene P Schulz by the way – so that's a Gerry surname but his Ma is a De Sallis – one of the Hampshire lot - so terribly good English background. This chappie gets to London just after Hitler moved in on Denmark and Norway – goes to their embassy here."
The Schulz surname was ringing a distant bell in Sir George's brain but he said nothing.
"Now I don't know if you are aware of the Yanks' top man here- chap called Kennedy - he seems to be taking neutrality rather too far."

Sir George was vaguely aware that the US Ambassador had been exhibiting some distressingly defeatist opinions so he had let "Mr Jermyn" continue:

"However, we do have friends at the Embassy and one of them tipped us off that there was an American who seemed very well up in in German aviation circles but was now wandering about England. So we watched him down in Hampshire and when he got back to London, I went to have a little chat. He bombarded me with technical stuff about jets and high temperature alloys which meant nothing to me – could have been just a blind but I thought you might be just the chap to check if he is the real McCoy. IF he is – then he could be useful. If he is working for the Nazis and trying to send us down a wrong alley – we'll deal with him. He's coming to your office tomorrow. Need hardly say this is all on the top side of Top Secret. I'll ring again day after tomorrow and you can tell me what you think."

So now the young man was in front of him.

"Please sit down" said Sir George though not with any warmth..

"Good of you to see me, sir."

"I fear I had little alternative" was the firm reply.

" I guess that would be your British Secret Service. They have been following me since I got into England from Sweden."

Sir G had no intention of wasting time. "Mr Schultz ... "he began.

"Call me Gene ..." came the interruption

"Mr Schultz. " Sir George continued firmly. "If you have information which might be of value to His Majesty's Government and you are prepared to divulge it – then pray proceed."

"Thank you, sir. I guess you know something of my travels."

"Mr Jermyn has indicated you have recently been in Europe."

"Correct sir."

"And how, may I ask, did that come about – given current circumstances?"

"If I may sir, let me give you something of a career raysumay" Though he deplored the young man's informal idiom, there was something about his manners which appealed.

"Please do". Sir George smiled for the first time. in the meeting.

"Like you, my Paw is a big cheese aviation-wise stateside."

Now Sir George remembered where he had heard the name.

"And he thought it would be a good idea for me to go to Germany as he reckoned they were setting the pace and I might learn and maybe bring some business. So off I go three years ago and I meet all the big guys – Ernst Heinkel, Willy Messerschmitt - and they are kinda glad to see me – Paw being who he is – a German name and me with a pilot's licence and over 300 hours certified airtime. And I get to see a lot and I take furloughs over in cute little Denmark and - gee I like that place - I was at a town I call El Senyor - you been there?"

Sir George shook his head.

"Then last summer I am back in Germany and in June I get to watch Mr Heinkel's rocket plane- then in August -a jet plane – boy was that a surprise! – but a couple of days later -- sure enough this little old European war breaks out and Paw says 'Get the hell outa there' . But I don't listen and go back to Berlin but I aint so popular there no more and have a miserable winter – not so much the war - more the weather. But everyone is telling me this war is about a load of little countries that don't really exist and why should the States be bothered. So come April, I head back north to Denmark but

I am no sooner in El Senyor again when the Germans walk into Denmark and me and my Danish buddy – we hear those bombers over Copenhagen, so we high tail it over a couple miles of water and into Sweden. And my Paw he wires me – 'this time you really get outa there -try to get to your kinfolk over in England'. And this I do on a little Swedish boat and boy is your North Sea a bumpy ride."

"It is indeed" agreed Sir George.

"So then I go down to my kinfolk in Hampshire County – no easy journey by the way. But I aint exactly welcome there. 'Join the RAF they say – fight for your Maw'. So I come back to Russell Square and then, outa the blue, a guy who calls himself Jermyn comes to see me. He grills me – boy was he good! He wanted to know how I mixed with the likes of Herr Heinkel and Herr Messerschmitt. So I kinda pointed out that my Paw is President of one big aircraft manufacturing corporation stateside and that's the sorta folk we mix with – even if we aren't exactly keen on their politics. So he buys this – or claims he does, you can't really tell with those guys – and tells me he'll fix up a meeting with some guy called Sir George something who is a big cheese here and I guess that's you."

"Well, I do have the title of Director of Advanced Projects" said Sir George though his voice still carried the surprise he had felt when called to the role. He continued firmly:

 "You realise young man, given your name and ancestry there may be some question as to which side you are on."

With the confidence of one who has had to make this explanation before, the young man stated equally firmly:

"My Paw – he likes to say we are all descended from a soldier in your King's German Legion who was captured in the War of Independence and kinda stayed on. That's some way off the truth! My folk came from Germany and headed to a place called Bismarck cause it kinda sounded right. But they didn't stick around for long before they headed for California which is where I'm from."

His fist pounded on Sir George's desk.

"Jees – I may have the Kraut name but – hell, my Maw is from your Hampshire County! My folks met in France in the last War. He was with Pershing; she was a nurse. He got wounded somewhere on the Hindenburg Line in 1918 – always claims it was an Australian not a German who got him. She nursed him - and you can guess the rest."

The young man took a deep breath.

"Now I've laid it on the line for you guys. Whether you believe me or not – I am going to volunteer for your Royal Air Force and fly one of these here Spitfires."

This changed everything for Sir G.

"OK – and I leave this with you – the Germans are splitting their efforts between rockets, pulse jets and turbo jets. I aint no gambling man, Sir George but if I were to be such, I'd put my dollars on these here turbojets but think hard about high temperature alloys. I don't think Uncle Ernst has got the answer but Uncle Willy might very well have. Now, you guys are on your own – or at least you will be till Uncle Sam comes to his senses to see off this Hitler. So you have a decision to make – but I guess you know that."

"You tell me you are going to volunteer for the RAF."

"Sure as God made little apples. And Uncle Sam can't get mad at me 'cos my Maw's sure 'nuff English – but we can always say I'm Canadian."

Sir George had by now warmed to this earnest young man – perhaps seeing in him something of the son he had never had.

"Well, before you do that, there are some people I want you to talk to. Are you prepared to spill the beans on rockets and jet planes and whatever you know on high temperature alloys?"

"Sure am – let's go!"

"We cannot do that directly - but within a few days. Can I ring you at your hotel?"

"I will surely attend on your call, sir."

The parting handshakes had warmth to them and as Sir George later stepped out into the streets of wartime London, there was a spring in his step which had not been there for months. He had been concluding that rockets were a thing of science fiction and pulse jets a mere toy. He would tell Jermyn on the morrow that the young American could be taken at face value. Then he would arrange to take him to see Whittle at Lutterworth and the people in Gloucestershire. He would tell Sinclair and the vulgar Beaverbrook that there would be a prototype jet fighter ready within – say – a year.

It had been a GOOD MORNING.

AUTHOR'S POSTSCRIPT

I shall let History take over from here and merely note that the RAF recognises 7 US nationals as aircrew personnel in the Battle of Britain but that several "Canadians" may have been US subjects. A prototype jet fighter, the Gloster E28/39 made its first flight within a year of the date of our little story.

MAY 1905

"Good morning, Sir George."

The words of Gillespie had been preceded by the respectful knock on the bedroom door and were accompanied by the accustomed rattle of a cup and saucer.

"It is a fine morning indeed, sir, for your trip to Glasgow," the butler said and, after laying the morning tea on the bedside table, he opened the curtains to prove his point. It was indeed a fine May morning and Sir George was rewarded with the accustomed view across Brodick Bay to the prominent pyramid-shaped peak of Goat Fell , Arran's highest summit. It was the view which had encouraged Sir George's father to expend a part of the family's fortunes derived from their Lanarkshire coalmines and construct a fine mansion on the south side of the bay which would be the family's summer base- a change away from their mansion on the braes south of Glasgow. Then, moving through into Sir George's dressing room, Gillespie called out to ask for confirmation that Sir George would be wearing his "Board Meeting in Glasgow "suit and that Lennox should bring the gig round to the front door at the usual time to drive him round to the pier to catch the 8.05 boat to Ardrossan.

"Your shaving things are laid out, sir. I stropped your razor yesterday" continued Gillespie, "and the maid will bring the hot water just the noo."

 Thus all had seemed well when, at the foot of the stairs, shaved and suitably suited, just as Sir George was turning to enter the Dining Room, Gillespie accosted his master.
"Lady Octavia is already at the breakfast table", he said with the raised eyebrows which suggested trouble lay in store.

Sir George had already sensed something different was afoot having heard his wife Octavia's maid, Ailsa, on the move earlier but had assumed it would be to attend to the two boys, his grandchildren, up from England and taking a short break – a few days on the island during their half-term. The trouble he sensed awaiting him on the far side of the Dining Room door would be to do with the fact that he had scarce seen them at all and that Lady Octavia had been seeing to their welfare.

She and Ailsa had met two excited young boys off the train at Glasgow Central Station. Now deemed old enough, they had travelled all the way up from England without a parent or Nanny, though with the Guard keeping a stern eye on them in their First -Class compartment. Instructed in a letter from their Grandfather, they had cheered when they crossed the Border and had, shortly after, listened to the beat of the engine struggling up to the summit of Beattock. Then they set to spotting the River Clyde, first in its youth winding out of the smooth green Lowland hills near Crawford as though to greet them, then as they crossed it at Uddingston where they knew their Grandfather had his coalmines, then again rumbling over the big metal bridge into the Glasgow terminus struggling with coats and luggage as they tried to get a glimpse of the shipping at the wharves. Feeling very grown up, they had walked down the platform accompanied by the Guard and the station staff – who well knew that these were the grandsons of one of the railway's directors here to meet the formidable figure of their grandmother duly attended by her maid.

His only meeting had been with two rather sleepy boys in dressing gowns that night after dinner [the rule of the house being 'never disturb Grandfather when he is busy'] who asked for permission for excursions: *"Please can Lennox drive us to Glenashdale waterfall tomorrow. Please can we have a trip on the fast boat and see the Atlantic?"*

That he had explained he would be unable to join them on their expeditions, he reasoned in rehearsing his defence, was not of his choice but arising from his business matters which had kept him in his study in which, of course, "Grandfather is not to be disturbed".

Matters had come to a head, for his company had to decide about sinking a new pit. Trial borings made in farmland in the north of Lanarkshire indicated workable coal seams but very thin - in that way typically Lanarkshire - but of excellent coking coal, so he would have no problem in getting his Board to agree the venture. There was a railway line close by from which a spur could easily be constructed and, as he was a Director of the railway company, did not envisage any difficulty. The new pit would need miners' accommodation nearby, so that had to be organised – 3 rows of miners' cottages and five substantial house, he thought -and his staff would have to start work on specifying a stationary steam engine to wind the coal.

On top of all that, he had a Board Meeting of the Railway Company with a substantial agenda whose perusal had taken him away from his grandchildren for yet another day.. These, of course, were matters he never discussed with his wife for, as his father, had schooled him, her domain was the house, the children, the kirk. But they would have to surface now, pausing before entering the Dining Room, if he were to fully explain his neglecting the boys and how he proposed to make up for that.

 "You are about early, my dear" he said, giving her a perfunctory kiss on the cheek. He took his accustomed seat at the other end of the dining table and both he and Lady Octavia paused their interchange whilst Gillespie served his master the habitual bowl of porridge.

"There are matters I wanted to discuss before you head off to Glasgow and your Board" began Lady Octavia but Gillespie with his trained butler's cough interrupted.
"Shall I ask Mrs Leckie to prepare a fresh dish of scrambled eggs?" he said, knowing full well that the resourceful cook would have anticipated the question and at that moment would be engaged in exactly that task. He continued:
"As I mentioned to Lady Octavia earlier, I much regret the bakers' boy is very late this morning."
"It will be that Catriona girl at The Lodge teasing him again" said Lady Octavia, showing she was up with local gossip.
"Or the Ballantyne's dog" grumbled Sir George, proving he was the equal of his wife in local knowledge.
"Thus we have no fresh rolls" continued Gillespie. "Will toasted bread suffice, sir?" And on being assured it would, he made his exit.

Sir George led: "If it is about the boys ...."
"Ach no" his wife replied strongly, "the boys are fine! We all had a grand day yesterday and the boys were with Lennox at the Glenashdale waterfall the day before!"
"I'm glad all that has worked out well". Sir George was being guarded, aware that something was brewing. But Lady Octavia needed to build up a head of steam first and decided to describe the previous day's expedition.

"As you planned, Lennox took us in the brake over to Lochranza. He is certainly a good driver and will make an excellent chauffeur I am sure. The road beyond Corrie is really rather rough but he handles the horse so well. Then we boarded the turbine and we were down in Campbeltown just after twelve. Annie took the boys to see the engines of course, but there seems to be little to see. She is really the most knowledgeable young lady. She explained to the boys that a turbine is like a windmill but with steam!"
"She has a brother on the boats" was Sir George's explanation for Annie's unexpected knowledge.
"Anyway, there was a sort of horse bus waiting for us and we went over to Macrihanish and the boys saw the Atlantic. The driver took rather a shine to our laddies and told them that looking out to sea the next stop is America!"
"True."
"Oh and of course, there's a colliery there of all places and the boys wanted know if it was grandfather's. And there's a wee railway and our driver said that next year it will go all the way to the Campbeltown pier and will take passengers. That will make a grand trip – if the idea ever comes off."
 "Indeed it will my dear and I fervently hope that I will have the time to take the laddies."
"You know they are heartbroken they have scarce seen you" was the reproachful reply but Sir George had planned ahead for this situation and had his response ready.

"I know, my dear and last night I arranged with Gillespie that I will take them myself to Glasgow and put them on the train to England. It is a midday service so we will cross on Duchess of Hamilton, then they can watch the engines and – if it is not too cold go right to the bow on the promenade deck.

And Captain Morrison may even allow us on the bridge. The we might have some few minutes in Glasgow and I can show them George Square or some such. Then, of course they will spirited back to that place in England where our son has chosen to exile them. Do please inform them that I will be taking them.”

“Och that will round off their wee trip just fine! But that is not what I wanted to talk to you about ..” Her voice tailed away for Gillespie had returned with a plate of scrambled eggs and a rasher of Ayrshire bacon that he set down before an appreciative Sir George who was much relieved that the boys’ welfare was not the subject of a harangue. Gillespie was very aware that he had interrupted something and decided that this should be his last appearance for some time.

“I am informed that the morning rolls have now arrived, Sir George. Will you be requiring some?”
Well aware that he would be probably repeating the current meal on arrival in Glasgow, Sir George indicated that he had no need.
“The boys will like them when they come down,” suggested Lady Octavia. “ They tell me they cannot get rolls or pies in England”
“It is indeed a heathen land,” opined Gillespie. “ Your bag is ready in the study Sir George, I understand. I will take it out to the gig which I see Lennox has brought round to the front. May I suggest the light overcoat.”
With that he retired.

Tucking into the eggs and bacon Sir George wondered what his wife had in store. If not about the boys, was it a repeat of the suggestion that they purchase an automobile? He was not to be left in doubt for long as his wife was now into her stride. "You are on the *Glen Sannox* this morning" she said, referring to the paddle steamer owned by the Glasgow and South Western Railway Company.

" Why use our rivals? Our *Duchess of Hamilton* is perfectly comfortable though I know you say *Glen Sannox* is faster. But why are the Caledonian doing nothing? What about these new turbine engines? I have it on excellent authority that last year the Board turned down the offer of turbine steamer."
"That was the Steam Packet Company. I am on the Board of the Railway Company" expostulated Sir George, aware that he was temporising.

"Och, that's a legal contrivance and you know it. If your Board tells the steamer people to do something they do it."
 "Our business is coal. I howk coal and sell it. It's good coal at a good price. All sorts of coal and wee bit ironstone as well. I turn the wheels of Scotland and I heat and light its homes."
"You have steam engines at your collieries. They wind the cages up and down the pits."
" But I am NOT a mechanical engineer. I rarely understand what the directors discuss - this business of the latest new express locomotive – I cannot follow them at all – but from what I gather it doesn't do what it's supposed on Beattock, so now we need another. So if the loco people get it wrong what about our steamship subsidiary? Are they not just being prudent and sticking to what we know and what we do well? I know all the talk is of these turbines but what is their cost? How much coal are they using to gain these unheard- of speeds?"

"George -this is shilly-shallying. You know that the Caley must put on a turbine steamer between Arran and Ardrossan. That Glen Sannox is indeed a beautiful ship but she is taking our passengers including you. George, we are a Caley family and I have Williamson blood in my veins. People talk. You have been spotted using St Enoch Station. No doubt splendid since they did it up but it is not OURS." Her Ladyship had reached a well-rehearsed climactic note.

" George – your using our rivals' boats and trains HAS to stop and the stopping starts now!" With that Lady Octavia swept from the room, almost colliding with an apologetic Gillespie who had returned to remind Sir George that it was high time he left to catch the steamer.

Seated beside Lennox in the gig as they trotted round the bay to the pier, Sir George could see his rival company's paddle steamer awaiting him. What a splendid sight she presented: her funnel was scarlet with a black top; the hull was light grey with dark red underbody; her paddle-boxes were white and glittered with much ornamentation; her deck houses were varnished teak and lifeboats were white with white covers. She was the epitome of speed and opulence but, having had time to reflect on the recent and most unusual domestic scene, Sir George's conclusion was: *Sorry, old lady but I am about to get you a rival!*

Later that day on the Caledonian Steam Packet Company's paddle steamer pounding across back to Arran. Sir George felt a degree of satisfaction. His time in Glasgow had concluded with his enquiring into the purchase of a motor vehicle and tomorrow he would be with his grandsons.

But in the morning, he had agreed the development of a new express locomotive, won the plaudits of the Board for his new coalmine in Lanarkshire and resulting new business for the railway and then – and he was looking forward to telling this to his wife – he got agreement to direct the steamer company to build a new turbine steamer and put it on the Arran run. "Yes" he thought. "A good lunch, an interesting afternoon but - most important - it was a GOOD MORNING."

AUTHOR'S POSTSCRIPT

In my search for an authentic background to the foregoing, I am indebted to Andrew Clark's masterful *Pleasures of the Firth- Two Hundred Years of the Clyde Steamers* [Stenlake 2015] and also his splendidly illustrated booklet: *Steamers to Arran* [Stenlake 2015]. Technical data came from A.J.S. Paterson's *Golden Years of the Clyde Steamers* [David & Charles 1969] which has for frontispiece a splendid colour tint of PS *Glen Sannox* in all her GSWR glory. Also useful was *Lanarkshire's Mining Legacy* Guthrie Hutton [Stenlake 1997]

In Clark's *Steamers to Arran* [p11] you may see both the vessels referred to in our tale and note that the author agrees with our Sir George's rating of the luxurious paddler.

Let us believe maybe, that Lady Octavia's nagging had some effect as, courtesy of Paterson [op.cit.], we can read in the CSPCo Minutes of 11-07-1905 *"Capt. Williamson [Coy Sec] instructed to get plans and approximate cost for the next meeting."* History tells us that the speedy turbine, *Duchess of Argyll,* began service on the Arran crossing the following year. [As did a narrow-gauge railway service in Kintyre.] To those erudite members of the Caledonian Railway Association [www.crassoc.org.uk] who so speedily corrected me when I seemed likely to transgress in an earlier publication, I would say *"This time, it's only a story"*

Dear Reader, you may still cross to Brodick and see one of Scotland's iconic views: that of Goat Fell and the Arran peaks. However, the crossing will take you longer than it did Sir George and it is difficult to recommend the current Ardrossan Ferry terminal.

OCTOBER 1932

"Good morning, Sir George."

The greeting came from the tanned and fit looking young man standing at the rail of **RMS** *Adda* bound from Liverpool to West Africa. Sir George, who, from previous short conversations knew the young man only as "Bobby", had not divulged any of his own personal details and was rather surprised to be addressed by his title.

He had taken some time to get his sea legs and when, still feeling distinctly queasy, he eventually ventured up on deck, had noticed the tanned, broad-shouldered young man with the ready smile who seemed happy to stand at the rail watching the sea go by.
"I had expected the weather to be warmer" said Sir George starting a conversation in the accepted English fashion.
"Och, it will be in a few days' time" came the reply.
"You're from Scotland?"
"Uddingston, near Glasgow. Originally. My family has moved to Stirlingshire."
"There seem to be a lot of Scots on this ship."
"You'll find us everywhere" came the reply with a smile.
"You sound like you've travelled this way before."
"I'm on my second Tour to Sierra Leone, so I'll be off at Freetown. I'm with the Development Company – we're opening up an iron ore mine - way up country at a place called Marampa. "
"I'm also bound for Freetown. I'm on business there. People to see. You are a Mining Engineer then?"

"Aye, passed my Surveyors' exams at Royal Tech. in Glasgow and then there were no jobs in Scotland. I'm Bobby."

"George.".

The two men shook hands.

"Now, if you'll excuse me, I must try to find my cabin steward."

"You're in the First Class?"

"Yes indeed."

"I travelled home First Class on this ship last July. Very grand."

"My first experience of ocean travel. Not a happy one so far, I'm afraid. You sound like an experienced traveller."

"Not really but I've sailed to Australia and then back."

"Mining?"

"Farming. Didnae work out."

"This must be working out, if you travelled First Class."

"These tours are all expenses paid and these Elder Dempster West Africa boats are quite small and don't have a lot of Second- and Third-Class berths. So there's no space by the time they get to Freetown and we have to go First Class. It's very nice!"

At which the two had gone their separate ways.

A few days later they met again by the ship's rail.

"You're looking a wee touch better" said Bobby by way of greeting.

"I think I'm getting those sea legs at last", replied Sir George.

"And of course the sea is a lot calmer. I'm getting about the ship a bit and managing to do justice to the excellent food. The ship is rather quieter than I expected."

"These ships are just transport to work – like the train into Glasgow Central in the morning. So the boys on here are

going back to their jobs – where it's hot and sticky – and a lot of them are leaving the wife and the weans."

"Are you?"

"Och no – I'm no married!" smiled Bobby.

"Some of you were trying to play cricket on deck. Unusual for a Scot."

"It's not unusual in Uddingston. All my family played for the local club. My Uncle Hugh – he was a fast bowler but he was killed in the War."

"I never realised it was so strong in Scotland."

"Och it is so! Uddingston once played against Gloucestershire."

Though that surprised him, it was said with such conviction, Sir George decided not to comment.

"Indeed! I played at school. Glad I did for I am sure that's how I got into Brasenose."

Seeing a look of puzzlement on the young man's face at the sound of the strange word, he explained: *"Oxford University. Didn't stay. Not an academic. Went into the family business. Travelled in Europe. Other than the Channel never sailed far."* He changed tack. *"You were sketching the other evening?"*

"Oh aye. I like to take the wee book with me. It's been to Australia and back."

"And there was a group of you having your picture taken."

"Aye. Last Saturday. My brother Johnny gave me a camera when I went to Australia and I still use it. I took some snaps of Marampa to show the folks at home. We got the Purser to take our picture. That's some of the boys from Marampa and our boss. They've done a few tours now. They're very good at winning the sweepstake on how far the boat travels in a day."

"That was a Saturday? I rather lose track of days on board."

""We sailed on a Friday. My eldest brother – he was on the Anchor Line -used to say that's unlucky."

"Unlucky for me – missed that weekend entirely– nobody told me how rough the sea is this time of year."

"I've known rougher – Indian Ocean on way to Australia- and a bigger boat too!"

"Is Adda a particularly fast ship. I see she is a motor vessel not a turbine."

"She's not as fast as the boats on the Clyde. The turbines there can do twenty knots. Adda might just manage fourteen."

"Ah yes – I've met your Clyde steamers. Very impressive. Honeymooned in Scotland. Before the War. Took a trip on the Clyde. Went to that island with the mountains."

"Arran"

"That's it. But we didn't do a lot on the Clyde. We hired a car. I remember the roads being very rough."

"Wait till you see them in Sierra Leone! But Scottish roads are a lot better now. And of course there's a lot more cars. Everyone seems to have one now. Mr. Brown at the local shop in Banknock where my family live now has got one – and his elder daughter drives it!"

"Sounds like she'd make a good wife for you, Bobby!"

And this quite inconsequential chat had comprised the total exchanges between them.

"You have found out my name" he said in surprise.

Bobby, in his easily identifiable Scottish accent explained: "I think I told you I had sailed on this ship before and I know the Purser. He told me who you are."

"You are clearly an enterprising chap", said Sir George who at that instant decided to come clean. "Do you have a few minutes?"

"I managed to have my bath early this morning so there's a bit of time before breakfast. I dinnae want to be late mind!"

"I have to tell you that I'm from the bank which has financed your Development Company."

"The Purser told me you were with a bank. I don't know much about Finance. My young brother is training to be an accountant but I can't follow those things. Should you not be talking to my boss then?"

"No, Bobby not just yet I was hoping you might be able to fill me in on a few things."

"Well don't take long now!"

"I'll try to be brief. I think I mentioned I was with the family firm before the War. Travelled a lot in Germany and so on. When War came they got me into the Intelligence Corps – I even made it to Haig's HQ. Met a chap who I think was that author who wrote Thirty -Nine Steps. Found I didn't really know Germany – could never remember the names of the towns – but I'd picked up a lot of idiom so I was quite useful with letters and so on. End of the War, Pater died, I was sole surviving son so I became 'Sir' George – rather embarrassing really but the Bank wanted me to join - so I did – pleasant enough life - met lots of chaps I had been to school with."

Sir George could sense some irritation in his young companion who had been glancing at his wristwatch and now asked: "So why are you going to Freetown?"

"My Bank is keen to see exactly what is going on at your mines. It is after all three years since we set up the Development Company."

"They're not really "mines". Not like the pits back home. There's a big hill full of haematite and we are going to quarry it. So we'll be taking the ore down to the railway and not like the coalmines where you haul it up to surface."

"Really? I don't think I'd realised that. I'm from the London office you see. Not actually into mining as such. But nobody from Edinburgh was available to come out - the 'White Man's Grave' they were calling it."
 Sir George had turned to face out sea and was gripping the taffrail with both hands.
"So – well life has been rather empty since my wife died – she never got over that Spanish 'flu and then losing our baby –it's only been the cricket that's kept me going."
He turned back to face Bobby, "I support Middlesex by the way .."
"Our family has always supported Lancashire " said Bobby, brightening.
"Good team. Good club. Anyway I volunteered to go and have a look at the operation and they must have thought – Intelligence Corps in the War – so probably can spot what's going on - though my doctor was dead against it. It was only after my passage was booked and I'd had those jabs that I discovered the reason nobody else would do the job was that the Bank's man in Sierra Leone had just died from malaria."
A by now embarrassed Bobby looked directly at the lean and melancholy older man.
"How is it I can help you?"
"What I cannot grasp is why it is taking so long. Why all this business with a railway when map shows there is already one there running out of Freetown? Why build a port when Freetown is there? I am assured this is a perfectly viable project but I've looked at a map and it looks like there is a perfectly good railway running into the interior. Your mine or quarry whatever is near a place called Lunsar – is it not ? – why not build a branch?"
Bobby assumed the patient expression he used when explaining matters to an Englishman.

"Yes - there is a railway but it's just a narrow gauge - like the line from Campbeltown to Macrihanish - it can't handle big trains with iron ore. And anyway you'd have to build a muckle bridge over the Rokel. And how could you get iron ore to the boats? When we get to Freetown, you'll see it's not like getting off the Arran boat in Brodick or Whiting Bay when you gang along a pier. We have to go ashore on a wee boat. Freetown's all hilly - there's nae place you can build an iron ore port with storage bunkers and loading gantry."
"Oh! I hadn't really grasped that!"
"So - as well as the mine workings we're building a railway. It's three- foot six gauge but the boys on that have done the same in India and Australia and we'll have these muckle great Garratt engines tae pull trains down to a place called Pepel. Everything has to come out from home but in a year from, now there'll be boats there taking iron ore back to Glasgow – and maybe I can get a sail home on one. I'm sorry but I'm away to my breakfast."

As the young man dashed away, Sir George felt a sudden sense of enlightenment and total relief. For the first time, he felt he knew what the project was about and he could make a show of expertise when he reached the Colony. He had endured some days of utter misery on the trip but, for the first time on his trip, he felt it was a **GOOD MORNING.**

AUTHOR'S POSTSCRIPT

The savvy reader or any of my kinfolk will very quickly have spotted that I have made up a story about a possible encounter of my Dad [R .S. Yule (1906-82)] on one of his Tours of Duty to Sierra Leone in the 1930's. My source is my book *Other Times, Other Places* [CompletelyNovel 2019] and so this is the one tale I can illustrate!

A group by the rail on ADDA, Saturday 8th October 1932. Dad [the Bobby of this tale] is on the right. Is that the boss in the middle? [Photo from Yule family collection]

Twin Screw Motor Vessel ADDA 7,815 g.r.t Launched 1921. Torpedoed and sank off Freetown 8th June 1941. 2 passengers +10 crew lost. [Photo From an Elder Dempster postcard in Yule family collection]

This would have been the sketch our "Sir George" saw Bobby making. [From the R S Yule Sketch book]

Marampa did start sending iron ore to Scotland in 1933 ... and of course Bobby DID marry Mr. Brown's daughter!

MAY 1943

"Good morning, Sir George."

The senior British Army officer, a man in his late forties with the crisp but amiable air of his rank - shown by the crossed sword and baton below a crown on his epaulettes to be that of a Lieutenant General - rose from his chair to welcome his visitor.

"I'm sorry" he continued. " I should have said 'Professor'!"

"No matter" came the rather breathless reply as Sir George sat on the proffered chair. Then, after hooking his furled umbrella on the edge of his host's mahogany desk, not without some effort he hoisted his bulging briefcase onto his knee. Under the Lieutenant General's curious gaze, he proceeded to open it and then, delving busily therein, extracted several packages which he piled onto his host's already crowded desk.

"I was a professor before I was given that "K" for helping Mr Baldwin and Mr Chamberlain. Now you see, I have here that which you asked me for at our meeting last month."

The Lieutenant General surveyed the carefully annotated packages with some alarm.

"I'm afraid I'm rather busy, Professor, you could have left that with one of my staff."

"Yes, your operation seems to have expanded somewhat since my last visit but I also wanted to have a further word with you."

"Indeed - I trust you had no trouble in picking up all those photographs."."

"None at all – thank you for making the arrangements."

 Sir George permitted himself a chuckle at the recollection. "What my neighbours thought when a military vehicle rolled up and I got in with two military policemen, I don't know! The same down in Kent, at my aged relative's, when they carried out the tin trunk with all my yachting stuff in it. I'd hoped to get as far as Ramsgate to see my laid -up yacht but it wasn't possible. So, here as per request, all the shots I have taken over the years of the French coast between the River Orne and the tip of Cotentin as you suggested at our first meeting."

That first meeting had certainly come as a surprise to Sir George. As he emerged from the taxi in London's St. James Square, carrying only his customary furled umbrella and with the obligatory gasmask case over one shoulder, he was rather sad to find that Norfolk House was not as he remembered. Number 31 was no longer the Georgian building but a modern multi-storey office block, looking like it had just been plonked down from Tavistock Square or some such. And now, with the sandbagged protected entranced and the windows criss-crossed with tape, it looked like many other similar premises across the capital.. Still puzzled by the rather peremptory summons to an urgent meeting which had come to him by telegram, he found, on entering, that it was a hive of military activity.

 Eventually he found himself being shown into to the office of a rather apologetic Lieutenant General who, it transpired, had requested the meeting. After a courteous exchange of greetings, apologies and pleasantries, Sir George could contain his curiosity no longer and directly enquired of his host exactly why he had been summoned.

The senior Army officer smiled: *"You have a Cambridge First in Natural Sciences."*
"Yes but that was many years ago."

"But now you are a professor and, I am told, you are a leader in your field."

"I am an economic geographer; I am a disciple of Weber."."
This last meant nothing to the Lieutenant General who continued: *"Some time ago you were consulted by Bomber Command."*

"Very true, but a schoolboy could have pointed out the economically important targets. But it was only a short walk round to Adastral House - unlike this morning. And I must confess, I cannot imagine why I am here – not that I mind – things are quiet on the academic front though I am doing my bit as an ARP Warden ."

"Professor, I must at this point remind you that you signed the Official Secrets Act."

"Ah – I see – this is something hush-hush."

"Distinctly so! In fact - you are here - and I am here because the Allied Powers intend to invade Europe and I am in charge of the planning for that assault."

"An awesome responsibility! But I cannot see my part in this ... although – in the last show I was involved in aerial photographical reconnaissance."

The Senior Officer continued: *"Planning is just beginning but I can tell you we aim to land an army on the shores of Normandy."*

"Normandy! I would have thought it most unsuitable! I've always assumed that at some point we might make an airborne landing in Pas de Calais and seize Calais and Boulogne from the rear."

Patiently, his host countered: *"I think you'll find the Germans have already thought of that! I hate to think what would happen to lightly armed paratroopers landing amongst a Panzer Division!"*

"Of course", agreed Sir George. *"You must forgive me! I live in a world where plans are not subject to enemy action!"*

"Without going into details",", continued the military man, *"we considered four sites for the landings. We settled on Normandy because the overriding consideration is that wherever we land must be within the range of our fighter aircraft flying from England."*

Sir George could see the point and nodded agreement but could see a difficulty.

"But there are hardly any ports on the Normandy coast", he continued. *"Surely Le Havre and Cherbourg are heavily defended."*

"I said 'the shores' and I understand you are a yachtsman and an acknowledged expert on the Channel coast."

"I was a keen yachtsman in peacetime and know the Channel pretty well. I still cannot see why I am here – surely you should be talking to one of the Free French."

"I need to talk to someone quite urgently who has specialist knowledge and whom I can trust not to mention a word of this conversation. I believe that is you, Professor."

"I'm honoured and indeed have contributed to numerous editions of Channel Pilot - yes - and added my own comments on the hinterland of the ports and harbours. But I've also sailed in East Anglia and across to Holland –once met that dreadful writer chappie Ransome who writes those books that encourage youngsters to go to sea on their own - but what is it about me you find special?"

"I am given to understand that you have the best private collection of photos of Normandy estuaries & harbours remaining in UK - all the rest seem to have been destroyed in the Blitz. I am particularly interested in .. let me check ..".

He opened a file on his desk which Sir George saw was prominently marked **TOP SECRET**.

" ... the shoreline between the mouth of the River Orne and the base of the Cotentin Peninsula." His voice took on a tone of anxiety:: *" Will you have something of that area?"*
"The answer is almost certainly 'Yes' but all my yachting papers went into a trunk when war broke out and are with an aged relative in Kent near Ramsgate. I understand, I need a special pass to go there."
The Lieutenant General thumped his desk with his fist: *"I'll arrange you a pass to Hell and back if necessary. Believe you me - this really IS the big one!"*

Thus it was, a month later, that Sir George had something of an air of triumph as he opened one of the packages and scattered a huge pile of large glossy photographs across the desk.

"May I explain?"

"Please do."

"What these photographs all show- and I've annotated them on the back and put in lat. and long. where I could - what they show are views of the French coast from out at sea – they show the landmarks a skipper has to look for to gain entrance to a harbour – so presumably – they would be useful to a pilot of an invasion craft. But I have to say - there are things they don't show."

"Tell me," said the rather surprised soldier.

"They can't show you the tides and in the Channel, the tide is king. Your people are going to have to know that. And there are numerous inshore hazards also – but you will get that from the Admiralty chart. For instance, from Lion sur Mer to a place called Arromanches there is an extremely dangerous rocky ledge called the Calvados Plateau - when I was younger, I once very nearly came to grief on it in a north-easterly on a falling tide."

"I am sure we will note it."

"And you must remember these ports are just very small fishing harbours."

"Does this remarkable collection include shots of the beaches?"

"Not as such but I can assure you there are miles of splendid beaches between the little estuaries. I am sure they will be admirably suitable for landing craft – though I suppose they are now all fortified."

"On behalf of my planning team, I must thank you.".”

"Glad to be of service, I seem to be of little use these days",", said Sir George, fastening his briefcase and preparing to leave, "but there is one thing I must mention – as a Geographer rather than a yachtsman."

"And what might that be?"

"Inland from those beaches, the country is what they call 'bocage'. It's mixed woodland and pasture, with fields and winding country lanes sunken between narrow low ridges and banks surmounted by tall thick hedgerows that break the wind but also limit visibility. It is the sort of landscape you get in parts of Devon. Not really very good for chaps in tanks! I rather think it would favour the German Army in defending it."

"I am obliged to you for that information. But – and I remind you that everything we have mentioned here is totally unrepeatable – I expect that we can gain surprise – and get well inland to a line Caen – Bayeux – St. Lo on Day One."

"You are the soldier, sir, not me!"

"I don't think we shall have to call on your services again, Professor",", said the soldier pointing to the mounds on his desk. "This will be a great help to us as there is going to be a major pow-pow shortly. Thank you very much indeed."

The meeting was clearly over and the Professor gathered his things ready to move, then, pausing and in the voice he used when emphasising a lecture point, he reiterated: "Remember –in the Channel. the tide is king" .
However before leaving the room , umbrella and briefcase in hand, he paused in the doorway:
"It sounds crazy, I know, but what you really need is to take the port of Dover and tow it across to Normandy!"

Back out in the select surroundings of St. James' Square once more, his briefcase now a light shell, Sir George found his initial elation at performing a simple but useful role had suddenly become overcast by doubt. Had he fully managed to convince his distinguished host of the difficulties an attacking army would face in the bocage country? He did not think so.. It had been foremost in his mind but the business with the photos had dominated the meeting. He clearly would have no future part in the secret work. What should he do? Write a letter perhaps? His mind now assailed by all manner of doubts he concluded that, after all he had not really had a GOOD MORNING.

AUTHOR'S POSTSCRIPT

I picked this episode in history because Dad, having acquired the skills of reinforced concrete construction at Marampa, was later called on to help build the Phoenix caissons which formed part of the Mulberry Harbours.

In seeking an authentic background to this tale, I consulted:
 D-DAY The Battle for Normandy Anthony Beevor [Penguin 2009]
OVERLORD D-Day and the Battle for Normandy 1944 Max Hastings [Pan 1984]
VICTORY IN NORMANDY Maj-Gen David Belchem [Book Club Assoc 1981]
D-DAY Warren Tute & others [Pan 1975]
 all of which helped me understand the colossal effort which went into the planning of D-Day and from which I learned that Lieut. General Frederick [later Sir Frederick] Morgan headed up a team that became too big for Norfolk House in October 1943.
Also the Fourth Edition of *The Shell Channel Pilot* Tom Cunliffe [Imrie Laurie Norie & Wilson 2002] reminded me of the nature of the Normandy coastline which I visited many years ago.

In worrying about the bocage country [US "hedgerow"], this Sir George certainly had a point. His suggestion of towing a port across the Channel was not such a crazy idea after all.

SEPTEMBER 2006

A minor drama in One Act for Five Voices and a SORP

<u>The Cast:</u>

Sir George	Chair of the Board of Trustees
Lady Alice	A Trustee of the Charity
Mr Jack Braithwaite	A Trustee of the Charity
Mr Neil Stirling	A Partner in an Accountancy firm
Ms Helen McMaster	An Audit Manager in the same

The scene is a Meeting Room in the Head Office of a firm of Chartered Accountants and Auditors, somewhere in London. It is eleven o'clock on a Friday morning and the three trustees are seated in glum silence when the Accountants come in.

Neil	Good morning, Sir George and lady and gentleman. My name is Neil Stirling. I am a Charity Partner here and with me is my colleague, Helen Mc Master, who is supposed to be your Audit Manager.
Trustees	Good morning
Sir George	Neil, Helen, thank you for arranging for us to use this room. If I can introduce - Lady Alice and Mr Braithwaite. Lady Alice is a founder trustee, as I expect you know and Mr Braithwaite has been bringing his business expertise to us for some years too.
Helen	I trust you have all helped yourselves to the coffee and biscuits provided.
Neil	Are we expecting anyone else, Sir George?
Sir Geo.	I'm sorry but at short notice it was impossible.
Neil	Then we will not be quorate – but no matter.

Lady Alice	I trust this is as urgent as George said it was. I've come all the way up from Godalming specially.
Jack	And I'm only here by chance as the lady wife has dragged me down from Yorkshire on a shopping trip. Our niece gets wed next month.
Sir George	Can we get to business please? Neil, I've already told them that, Mr Keane our Chief Executive has resigned ...
Jack	.. and about bloody time, too! Total nutter on an ego trip! Not on t' same planet as us!
Sir Geo.	Jack please!
Lady A	Mr. Braithwaite your rudeness is the reason people do not attend these meetings.
Jack	Wrong, Lady Alice! Trustees don't bother coming because all that happened is that Keane rabbited on for an hour about how good he'd been and what wonderful things were going to happen – and you've not been around for a year George – so he got away with it.
Lady Alice	But he has done such wonderful work. He raised so much money - all these wonderful grants.
Sir George	To be fair Alice, his wife – or rather his ex-wife - did the hard work getting those grants – she is an expert at it. She runs a consultancy. But I have to say at the outset, that I take the blame for much of what has happened. As you know I was asked to go to the USA for a year and the opportunity was too good to turn down. I realise that I have neglected my duties and if it is your wish I shall resign also.
Lady Alice	Never! We all realise that you are at the very top in your profession. We are so lucky to have such a famous person. Please stay!

Jack	George – now that idiot Keane is out of the way, this charity needs you at the top more than ever. If you go -I go. I'm here because the lady wife insists on it but I've made a habit of not being associated with failure. And - from where I stand - this here is failure.
Sir G	So be it - I shall stay – for now anyway
Jack	First things first Mr Charity Partner – has Keane had his fingers in the till?
Neil	Mr. Braithwaite. As far as we can tell - no!
Helen	Given that your financial records are – to the say the least – incomplete, we have not found any evidence of irregularity.
Jack	I'm right glad to hear that! And call me Jack, please!
Lady Alice	Then why has our inspiring Chief Executive resigned? And why – suddenly - is there something wrong with the money records when we have that lovely girl Annie? You are not accusing her surely? And what about our treasurer – the Welsh wizard – Reverend Thing – you surely cannot accuse a man of the cloth! We never had this unpleasantness until you insisted we needed accountants, George!
Sir G	Alice, please! Can we take this in order please – Neil can you go over the points we raised with Keane on Wednesday?
Neil	Let us just report what has happened – Helen, can you start with Tuesday please.
Helen	Sir George and I had a meeting at the office – Mr Keane was away somewhere ..
Jack	He's always out! You never catch him in. Gave up trying years ago.
Helen	We spoke to Annie and Mrs Zadowi, who very kindly trotted in from Cricklewood. Actually she brought files full of records and said she'd

had enough of working with you! As I see it, everything was fine and dandy when you were a wee charity in that   office over the Indian Restaurant in Willesden Lane ...

Lady A   Such inspiring days!

Helen   ... and Annie took the bills to Mrs Zadowi over in Cricklewood who wrote the cheques and did the wages once a month. Annie was in tears, so she was. She never pretended to understand accounting – she was hired to answer the phone, run errands, do the post, type a few letters and make the tea and so on.

Jack   And now you're in a complete floor just off Gray's Inn Road – and we must have millions by now!

Helen   We also spoke to the two other staff you have – Cameron and Khamenei –

Jack   Only two? There's more than that in the office!

Helen   Surely, but they're mostly volunteers – only two are on the payroll – believe me – and neither have ever had a Contract of Employment and they don't really know what their jobs are – they get a payment monthly from Mrs Z but she only guessed what their salaries are.

Jack   This goes from bad to worse!

Helen   True – there IS more! Yesterday I did finally make contact with your Treasurer. He is difficult to follow on the telephone but he is quite clear that he resigned a year ago.

Sir G   He sent me a letter which I got just before I left for America... but is was in WELSH. I didn't have time to get it translated – God knows who would have done that anyway.

Neil   On the face of it, you certainly have plenty of cash in the bank. But much of that is from the large grants Mr Keane and his wife obtained – a remarkable effort, I have to say. ..

Lady A As I keep telling you...

Neil .. but that money has very largely not been put to the use for which it was granted. Unless it is – and you can prove that - most of your funders will freeze further payments or want the funds returning and then you will REALLY be in financial trouble. Helen has had a look at the projects you are supposed to be running ..

Helen .. indeed I have! For example now - the YOSOH project -"Young Shoulders – Old Heads" –

Lady A Inspiring idea!

Helen I'm here to tell you, we can find no evidence of that project ever starting and 'tis not the only one!

Neil We put all this to Mr. Keane on Wednesday when we finally ran him to earth. He blamed everybody but himself to start with – then Sir George read the riot act and I informed him of his legal responsibilities. At that point, the fella broke down and explained his marriage had collapsed and he was actually living in the office- not a pleasant scene at all. Upshot was that he resigned there and then.

Jack I wondered if there were summat wrong there.

Lady A I am deeply sorry to hear that such an inspiring man should have such troubles. But they will not be helped by all this insistence on having these impudent accountants! How dare they summon us here and pin badges on us ! We do not run the charity; we are not managers – why are you troubling us with all these matters?

Sir Geo.	Alice – patience – please! Neil - it might be a good idea if you read out what you read to me on Thursday – the Charity Commission thing.
Neil	I brought it along, Sir George, and its correct name is "Statement of Recommended Practice" we call it the SORP.
Sir G	Tell us those important bits then.
Neil	Let me read: *Your charity's annual report and accounts not only help you manage your charity well by recapping on the achievements of the past year but can help you attract money from organisations or people who are interested in what you do. The annual report and accounts together form a package that provides accountability to stakeholders in the widest sense.*
Lady Alice	"Accountability"? "Stakeholders"? This is accountants' gobbledegook!
Neil	I read on, Lady Alice: "*The whole purpose of your charity's annual report and accounts is to demonstrate to your funders, donors, beneficiaries and suppliers in an open and transparent way, how you have spent the money you have received, how what you have spent supports your work and the resources available to you at the end of your financial year.*"
Lady Alice	How can anybody doubt our good faith! Remember it was my money started this charity! And why was I not warned about all this when we set up in Willesden Green?
Sir George	To be accurate it was your family trust who funded us and me that applied for us to be a charity and we **WERE** told about the requirements - Neil I'm sure it's in your handbook.

Neil	Let me conclude: *Every registered charity is expected to produce an annual report and accounts that explains where your money came from and what you did with it.* I repeat, Lady Alice – *expected to produce an annual report and accounts.* This charity has not yet done so. And now you have reached a stage where your income is such that you have to report to the Charity Commission and in the manner that they "Recommend".
Lady Alice	But that woman - Mrs Thingy - that Annie sees has always given us a list of the cheques she drew up and the dear Reverend would show us the bank statement.
Jack	He would wave it in the air like Chamberlain back from Munich, you mean! And then he'd thank God - in Welsh!
Neil	That is not what the Law requires Lady Alice!
Lady A	This SORP thing is law!
Neil	It is the law relating to charities.
Jack	Wish I'd known about this earlier George!
Lady A	This is impertinence – you are only accountants. As far as I'm concerned, like the chimney sweep - you come in once a year do a job and go – I know this from my family – our accountant – does the tax thingy every year – tells what to do to avoid paying too much tax and that's it – none of this hectoring and sorping! Preposterous!
Neil	We may be but humble accounting folk, Lady Alice, but we have a professional responsibility and all of you have a legal responsibility as charity trustees, which you seem to have overlooked, and I am trying to point that out as gently as I can.

Lady A   This is a conspiracy to reduce all our work to nothing more than pages of totally incomprehensible numbers! Soulless bureaucracy! I for one want nothing more to do with this! I didn't start this charity to be preached at by you young people with your silly SORPS– and I'll have no more of it. George I thank you for everything you have done but this is the parting of our ways. You are welcome to your boring accounting world!
A chair scrapes. A door bangs as she EXITS

Sir G   I must apologise for that – I can assure you that any implied slur on your profession would not be echoed by myself or Jack or the other Trustees ...

Jack   .. and they'll stay on I'm sure so long as George is around – they like associating with fame.

Neil   I hear what you say but now - clearly you need as a matter of urgency – an interim Chief Exec.!

Jack   How do we find one of them?

Neil   They exist, I can assure you. We can put you in touch with a firm who specialise in finding them. And we can get you a Treasurer too.

Helen   You also need a properly qualified person to produce three years' Report and Accounts and you need a proper accounting system – you've actually had a grant which will pay for one.

Sir Geo   This we must get and we will rely on your guidance – but we will need someone to work it.

Jack   What do you propose to do about Annie?

Helen   When we spoke to her, we asked if she would want to stay if she didn't have to do anything with the finance side and – given her record here - she knows more about the business than anyone - we suggested that stay as PA to the new CEO – and she was really happy with the idea.

Jack And pay her properly for it too?

Neil Of course!

Jack Well now, this whole charity business is far better organised than I ever knew! So I reckon it's about time I put my money where my mouth is – so to speak. Can I suggest summat?

Sir G We're all ears, Jack!

Jack I can sort two problems: first – I will get my granddaughter Kaylee – she's a solicitor - to come in and sort out proper contracts of employment and owt else that needs doing legally. And if that Keane starts playing up then she will certainly sort him. OK?

Sir G. Sounds admirable – I am sure we accept that offer. We will pay her fees of course.

Jack Second -and at risk of this becoming a family business - we will lend you my other granddaughter, Hannah. She's recently qualified as an Accounting Technician and she can come in and help set up a proper computer accounting system. Well keep paying her salary – it'll be champion experience for her.

Neil That being the case I think we can lend you Helen to produce Reports and Accounts for the last three years. We will have to bill you for that though!

Helen Sure and that'll be a grand challenge too!

Jack And one more thing – I think it'd be best if I were be at the office next week to keep an eye on things till we get a CEO – is that OK?

Sir G Can't think of anyone better, Jack!

Jack It means I can stay down here at my club and get away from the lady wife and her sister and this damned wedding!

Neil	I think that concludes our business, Sir George. I rely on you to update the remaining trustees. I will initiate everything from our end. Helen and I will have to go but please stay and help yourself to another coffee.
Jack	Thanks very much, Neil and Helen.
Sir G.	I promise we will work much closer in future.
Jack	Neil, is that a Rosslyn Park tie you're wearing?
Neil	It is indeed. I've been a member for years.
Jack	Is your First Team at home tomorrow?
Neil	Yes. Kick off three o'clock. I shall be there.
Jack	Champion. I shall be there. Good excuse to get away from the lady wife and her sister. Let's meet up in the bar afterwards and we can talk some details.
Neil	I shall look forward to that.
Sir George	I can't tell you all how relieved I am. I know we will get back on track now. Lady and Gentlemen, I think we have had a GOOD MORNING.

Exeunt omnes. Curtain etc.

AUTHOR'S POSTSCRIPT

You have been reading or listening to an entirely fictional playlet from a retired Charity Accountant and former resident of London NW2 who was a regular in an Indian restaurant in Willesden Lane. Written in affectionate memory of times spent in the company of members of the [then] Charity Finance Directors Group none of whom ever, of course, found themselves in quite the plight of the Accountants depicted here.

MAY 1752

"I bid ye Good morning Sir George."

At the greeting, Sir George turned in his chair by the coal fire where he had been sharing a pipe of tobacco and conversing with his guest, the seafaring man seated opposite him in the room high above the crowded streets and alleys of Edinburgh. He regarded his visitor with distaste for he saw in the doorway, a dishevelled sickly- faced youth who would now face a reckoning for the trouble he had caused his kinsfolk. Matters had come to a head two days prior when Sir George had a surprise visit from his distant kinsman Ebenezer Balfour of Broughton.

That the reason for the visit should be the conduct of young David was no surprise but Ebenezer's robust and welcome solution seemed appropriate to Sir George and he readily agreed to his visitor's stratagem. Thus it was both men met later with their business confederate Captain Hoseason and carefully laid plans which seemed to be fulfilling their intent with the arrival of the youth at Sir George's door.

"I am but lately roused by Mistress Macrae with tidings that I must immediately attend upon you" announced the youth.

 "You have not mended your tardy ways, Master Balfour", began Sir George. "My man brought notice to Mistress Macrae yestere'en. But ye are here and on your own account, which is a good thing, I own, and perhaps a portent, for what I have to say to ye is of the highest import."
Sir George drew deeply on his pipe and then launched himself into a speech he had been preparing for some time.

"I promised that good man your father as he lay dying - dying I am sure of the wounds he received in the late rebellion -

that I would protect both you and your sainted mother -God bless her memory, who so quickly followed her man to the grave. On her deathbed that honest man your kinsman, Ebenezer Balfour of Broughton, similarly swore to be guardian unto ye. He saw to your schooling – you gave him little reward there – he set ye into an honest apprenticeship wherein ye have been nought but trouble and he found ye a bed in this toon with that good lady Mistress Macrae- to whose house ye have brought nought but disgrace. There is not a tavern in all Edinburgh that ye have not frequented and where ye have participated in every manner of licentious behaviour. Further, ye have kept company with persons of the Jacobite persuasion including one pockmarked fellow who may be the most wanted villain in all the realm."

Sir George took a puff on his pipe and continued:

"Balfour of Broughton has despaired of ye, so he and I are resolved upon a course to save your immortal soul. We met yestere'en with my friend and companion in trade Captain Hoseason, and this is he, and we are agreed that it is our Christian duty to rescue ye from that pit of vice into which ye have fallen. "

At that point, the youth made as to protest but Sir George was not for interruption.

"You will hear me out sir! "

 "I fear I am faint, Sir George" cried the youth. "May I beg a seat?"

"Ye will stand sir, to hear yer doom at my hands" roared Sir George. "Yer kinsman and I are of a mind that ye be put to honest toil away from temptation and we are complicit with Captain Hoseason, who is master of our brig Catriona- and no more upright and Christian gentleman will ye find upon our coastal seas - that ye are to set sail with him as part of his crew this very day on his voyage in the salt trade to our northern towns. Else, Master Balfour, ye will be cast out as a beggar on the streets - for no more Balfour siller will come yer way. What say ye?"

"'tis a choice but no choice, sir."

"So Hoseason, you see the wretch before you - will ye take him to be a seaman?"

"I fear Sir George that he is but a weakly specimen who may not presently be put to the trade of seaman - but I am with ye in the matter of his salvation and consider that we may take him as cabin boy that he may duly bend his disposition to a more Christian character and erstwhile learn the ways of the sea trade."

"Capital. Capital! Now where is that splendid man Arneil? Ah here he is!"

The powerfully built serving man had appeared in the doorway, a stout leather bag in one hand, a cudgel in the other.

"You have Master Davie's bag?"

"Indeed, Sir George, and the widow Macrae has been well recompensed with Balfour siller."

"That is good. Now mak sure this young rascal does not leave your sight till he is well aboard the Catriona .. and watch his tricks mind."

"My enforcer is in hand Sir George – have nae fear of that!"

"I wish ye fair winds and a prosperous voyage, Hoseason and take extra care. The intelligence is that the Highlands are once more in a ferment after this cowardly murder in Appin – Campbell of Glenure – a decent, able man by all accounts, bending his endeavours to a difficult job. A young wife and two bairns to boot! A culprit must be found at all costs -at any cost! I hear that the Sheriff of Perth has issued a warrant for the arrest of Stewart of Ardshiel and yon pockmarked villain, Allan Breck Stewart. Pray God Hoseason, that we will root out this nest of vipers once and for all, that Scotland may go forward and that a new Edinburgh may spring up over on the Lang Dykes."

"Amen to that Sir George" replied the seaman. "But rest ye assured the towns of our north eastern coast and my own northern isles are seldom troubled now by Jacobite iniquities. With God's blessing, our trade shall prosper and this wild laddie come to his senses."

Bidding all a farewell, a satisfied Sir George concluded: "Mind now that Davie does not escape your charge and find himself amongst wild highlanders. Gentlemen, I bid you GOOD MORNING".

CODA

For our tale to be complete, we hear must about subsequent events so here , Dear Reader, is the rest.

It transpired that David Balfour did not like the sea and the sea did not like David Balfour. Far from making a man of him, the trip on the brig *Catriona* reduced him to a seasick invalid curled up in the bowels of the vessel and of no use to Hoseason and the crew. At the first opportunity the hapless youth jumped ship and found his way ashore at a northern port. His absence was not noted until well into the following day when a search of the vessel proved fruitless and Hoseason was forced to conclude young Davie was lost overboard, presumed drowned. Hoseason hailed a passing vessel, the *Covenant,* bound for the Firth of Forth and giving tidings of the loss in a message that its captain was asked to convey to Balfour of Broughton. Thus it came to pass that Ebenezer met up with a seafaring man in the Hawes Inn at South Queensferry to learn to his great sorrow that his plan to reform the reprobate youth had seemingly tragically misfired.

Meanwhile, young Balfour was making his way southwards across a Scotland which seemed like a foreign land to him. Begging and stealing food and sleeping in barns, he was twice arrested by soldiers on suspicion of being the Jacobite Alan Breck Stewart but quickly released. Finding the bridge over the river Forth at Stirling guarded, he headed through the Hillfoot towns to Inverkeithing where he persuaded a girl to row him over the Firth to Leith. Landing there, he was arrested to a third time but on this occasion was taken to Edinburgh Castle. However, he managed to persuade his jailer to contact our Sir George who secured his release and, rejoicing, took him to Balfour of Broughton, a man now broken in sorrow who was, as one might expect, overjoyed at the return of the prodigal. The young man had by now seen the error of his ways and so all lived happily ever after.

AUTHOR'S POSTSCRIPT

Named from its location, a coastal district of the West Highlands of Scotland, what is known as the "Appin Murder" occurred on 14th May 1752 some six years after the suppression of the last Jacobite Rebellion. The spot where Colin Campbell of Glenure was shot in the back is marked today by a cairn. The resulting trial and execution of James Stewart is widely seen as a notorious miscarriage of justice and has attracted a deal of literature, factual and fictional, the best known of the latter being Robert Louis Stevenson's novel *Kidnapped.* which was first published in the magazine *Young Folks* from May to July 1886, and as a novel in the same year.

Son of a noted lighthouse engineer, Stevenson was born in Edinburgh in 1850, his mother's maiden name being Balfour. His maternal grandfather, Lewis Balfour, was a minister of the Church of Scotland at nearby Colinton and we are told that Stevenson spent the greater part of his boyhood holidays in his maternal grandfather's house

In concocting this tale, I am obliged to *Walking with Murder: On the Kidnapped Trail.* Ian Nimmo [Birlinn Ltd. 2005] and also to my late Mum, Anne Copland Yule, for passing on her Tusitalia 1923 Edition *of Kidnapped* [complete with map of David Balfour's supposed travels]. From that work, I quote:

"PREPARATORY NOTES BY MRS R L STEVENSON

My husband was always interested in this period of his country's history and had already the intention of writing a story that should turn on the Appin murder. The tale was to be of a boy, David Balfour, supposed to belong to belong to my husband's own family, who should travel in Scotland as though it were a foreign country, meeting with strange adventures and misadventures by the way."

Thus RLS could *maybe* have heard my tale of a wayward ancestor's redemption at his Grandfather's knee and later embroidered it into an adventure story, altering the character of the participants, adding a romanticised picture of Allan Breck Stewart, and tying it into the events in Appin.

With apologies for treading on hallowed ground to the RLS Club [www.robert-louis-stevenson.org/rls-club] and the numerous societies worldwide who celebrate the life and works of Scotland's greatest storyteller.

JANUARY 1920

"Good morning, Sir George."

Sir George felt quite honoured that the only other occupant should greet him as he boarded the First- Class Carriage at Oxford station. This was especially so as he had not, for some time on this London train, encountered the slightly built man with the prominent cranial domes and a distinguishing lump on the forehead above the left eye – presumably arising from some accident - whom he had first met under very different circumstances but recognised now as an acclaimed author. He was delighted to meet again as he had hankered on passing an idea to the writer and this would be possibly his last chance. More to his satisfaction, as the train pulled out of the station, the two were to be the only occupants of the compartment that morning.

That first meeting had occurred in the same location but on a bleak morning the previous December when the two had come together, making typical remarks about the weather and then recognising they had met before.

"Colonel Buchan?" enquired Sir George.

"My goodness", his companion had replied. *"It is some time since I was addressed in that form."*

"That was your rank when I met you last! It was at Haig's HQ in '16."

"It was somewhat thrust upon me. One has to have rank in the Intelligence Corps. I was happy enough with 'Major' but Lieutenant Colonel it had to be. I remember our meeting because we had met before – in South Africa. You were quite the dashing soldier in those days."

"Those days are passed now. I have the family estate in Ayrshire to run and our coal-mining business to supervise."

"But you are clearly doing neither here!"

"Indeed I am not, Colonel Buchan .."
"... Please, I am JB to my friends!"
"Then 'JB' it is. You are correct I am presently a 'Blawn awa'
Jock'. I was brought onto the Board which is setting up our
new War Museum of which you must have heard."
"Indeed yes and I am much perturbed that there are those
who raise their voices against it."
"That will come to naught, there will be an Act of Parliament
next year. But it requires my continued presence in
London."
"As does my work with the publishers and also Reuters."
"You may well be used to it but – you will remember from
South Africa long ago – I am not a city man. It is enough that
I have to travel regularly into Glasgow."
"A fine city, I lived there and went to school there! I was very
worried by the disturbances earlier this year."
"So, for my sister here in Oxford, knowing my distaste for
London, there was nothing for it but that I stay with her for
the duration and take this train up to London."
"I find the trip provides me with welcome thinking time."
"I find it a welcome break! My sister's academic world is not
for me either. I an open spaces man. I often wish I were back
on the veldt."
"You are not alone there", replied the author, wistfully.
The English convention of not speaking in railway carriages
having been broken by two Scotsmen, the conversation
turned to recent affairs, the unrest in Scotland, the
disturbance in George Square at the start of the year and the
arrest of the ringleaders.

The pair had parted on reaching London, both expressing
the hope that thy would meet again but until this morning
chance had ordained that not to happen.

"Good morning JB" replied an emboldened Sir George, taking his seat. "I have not seen you for some time."

"Susie and I and the family have finally moved. Did I tell you we spent all last year looking for a place? Eventually we settled for the Manor and purchased last November but there was so much to do, we have been renting in Headington, which is where I was last December when we last met."

"The new place is to your liking?"

"It is ideal. I can see us being there for years to come. And Elsfield is not too far out of Oxford, so it is no problem for Webb to run me down to the station in the morning. How is your new museum coming along?"

"All goes well I'm happy to report. In fact my contribution regarding exhibits is now complete. So today will possibly be my last trip into town. I shall be glad to get back to Scotland and I think my sister will be glad to see the back of me. We have really drifted apart. She has lost touch with her Ayrshire roots I'm sorry to say."

"And the museum?"

"I am pleased to say it will open this summer and His Majesty himself will do the honours. May I ask if you are busy with one of your tales at present?"

"I am always busy with publishing and news reporting. Why do you ask?"

"I have a small tale which may interest you."

"Pray reveal it."

"There is a man of my acquaintance, a Gregor Dickson– he worked in one of our collieries and then came into money somehow and bought a public house – though he describes himself in a more genteel fashion as a "Wine and Spirit

Merchant". I met him by chance in Glasgow back home in Scotland over the New Year, and he told me that he has now retired from the Licensed Trade and last summer he took into to his head to go on a walking tour. I know him to be a great man for walking - in his time he thought nothing of walking three or four miles to the pit and back each day - and he decided on a coastal walk in Carrick and Galloway. That is country you know well, I believe."

"Indeed I do. Wonderful country. I walked and climbed there when I was a student."

"I think he picked it because it was close at hand - he is not a great man for train travel and getting to the Highlands would involve just that - excellent though our railways are - or perhaps were - the War hit them hard too."

"As it did all Scotland. We have yet to see the final reckoning."

"Ah yes, as we have remarked before - but 'tae oor tale' - as Burns said. Our Mr. Dickson is well into his solo excursion - by the way, he took for a walking stick the Irish cudgel he used as a publican to settle arguments - and he is somewhere along the coast of Carrick."

"Aha - a wild and lonely place."

"Surprisingly so! And he is just crossing a burn in a wee glen that runs down to the sea and he spies a gang of youngsters who seemed to be camping there and they saw him with his pack on his back and one of them shouted: 'Haw see the auld man gaun tae the schule!' - at which he could easily tell they were from Glasgow. You may not have encountered the Glesca keelie ..."

"Oh indeed I have! Being a son of the manse, I was once persuaded into leading Sunday School classes for Gorbals boys. I often thought that much might be made of them. The

War proved that, I think, - though by now there must be a new generation."

Sir George's narrative was interrupted. An intrusion of smoke and smuts from the locomotive required the closing of windows and no sooner had he resumed his seat than the Guard, with the politeness he reserved for First Class passengers, looked into the compartment to enquire about the possession of tickets.

"Well, you will understand that insults are not to Mr. Dickson's liking," continued Sir George eventually, "and he was about to remonstrate forcibly with these laddies when another appeared over the rim of the glen shouting: 'Quick it's the tinkers'. Then suddenly there appeared half a dozen ruffians who appeared set on chasing off the wee laddies. That seemed rather unfair to Mr. Dickson who immediately took the laddies' side in the matter and, waving his cudgel, rushed into the fray. Now, as I said, he is a stockily built man and one who could keep order in a coalminers' pub. So I can believe him when he said that the tinkers did a swift about turn."
" A Bailie Nicol Jarvie moment" enthused the writer.
"Indeed yes" replied Sir George, recognising his intellectual companion's literary reference. "Well, that's where Dickson's tale ends but I think he might well have kept in touch with those laddies and I know him to – secretly – be a generous man. I just wondered if you might like to use this wee tale somewhere."
The writer was suddenly lost in thought. Then he brightened: "It so happens that MacLean has been badgering me to produce one of my Shockers for his so-called Popular

Magazine. It has to be an adventure in serial form. So maybe I can use your miner-turned-publican as a hero."

"You would change the name of course?"

"Indeed and – as a son of the Manse – he could not be a publican! I could make him something very humdrum – a humble grocer say. And your episode could show how thin is the divide between civilisation and barbarism. We can have something of the Bolshevik menace about it perhaps your tinkers might be acting as their agents."

By now Sir George was beaming and the writer continued:

" I am obliged to you for passing on that tale and indeed it could well the be mainspring of an adventure story. In fact, I am sure it will."

Thereafter the two fell to discussing matters of the moment and talk of the current crisis in Ireland filled the conversation till Paddington.

Arriving at the London terminal, Sir George bid a fond farewell to his travelling companion and although he was back in a city he hated, he felt light-heated, for this would be his last such trip. He had been successful in acquiring the exhibits he had wanted for a new national museum, so he would not have to stay with his sister in her academic ivory tower much longer. He would soon be back in Ayrshire walking the dogs on the family estate but most of all, a famous author was going to include one of his stories in a new work and that would indeed be something to point out to his sister and her intellectual set.

It was indeed , he decided, a GOOD MORNING.

AUTHOR'S POSTSCRIPT

Sir George's "JB" is, of course, none other than John Buchan , 1st Baron Tweedsmuir of Elsfield, [1875 -1940] scholar, poet, journalist, author, soldier, country landowner, politician, diplomat and eventually statesman as Governor General of Canada. In learning about this remarkable Scotsman, who was clearly much more than just the author of *Thirty- Nine Steps,* I consulted:

John Buchan and His World ; Janet Adam Smith [Thames and Hudson1979]

John Buchan: The Presbyterian Cavalier; Andrew Lownie [Thistle 2013]

Beyond the Thirty -Nine Steps Ursula Buchan [Bloomsbury 2019]

The Flowers of the Forest, Scotland and the First World War Trevor Royle [Birlinn 2006] esp. Chap 12 *Aftermath*

To the best of my knowledge, my broad-shouldered Great Grandfather, John Train Scott, [*photo from the Yule Family collection*] the ex-miner and landlord of the Clydesdale Arms between Motherwell and Wishaw, never went on a walking trip but certainly described himself as a "Wine & Spirit Merchant".

One can easily imagine that type of personality as quite able to terrify a gang of tinkers!

From Aug to Sep 1921, John Buchan's *Huntingtower* was serialised in *The Popular Magazine.* We cannot tell if our Sir George read that magazine but it was published in book form in 1922 and so he would have rushed to purchase a copy and read of the exploits of retired grocer Dickson McCunn and the Gorbals Die-Hards.

I have imagined our Sir George to be a member of Sir Alfred Mond's Committee – or one of its many sub-committees – whose task was to collect material for what would become the Imperial War Museum, opened by HM King George V on 9th June 1920 on its first site at Crystal Palace.

.. and APOLOGY

My apologies to The John Buchan Society (http://www.johnbuchansociety.co.uk) for trespassing into their camp by the Garple Burn and hoping they will not send a retired grocer and some Glasgow laddies to chase me off. In mitigation, may I plead that *Thirty- Nine Steps* and *Greenmantle* have long been on my shelves together with a copy of the Nelson's edition of *Huntingtower* . That last I inherited from my maternal grandfather, Andrew Brown [junior] of Hollandbush, Banknock, a humble grocer by trade but one who had attended Hutchesons' Grammar School in Glasgow which, of course, was also the *alma mater* of JB.

JANUARY 1930

"Good morning, Sir George."

Thus addressed and laying aside a day -old English language newspaper, Sir George arose from his comfortable armchair in the lounge of the Cairo hotel to meet his expected visitor who was being directed across the quiet room by an obsequious hotel employee.

"Mr. Ransome," was his greeting as the two shook hands. "Something of an honour to meet you. I have studied much of your work. Pray make yourself comfortable. Something to drink?"

Sir George found himself looking at a rather donnish sort of chap such as one might meet walking around an Oxford quad; not a foreign correspondent who had hobnobbed with the leaders of the revolution in Russia and who had married one of their secretaries! A man who would not stand out in a crowd of office workers crossing London Bridge of a morning on their way to their City desks and not someone who had recently travelled to strife-torn China!

"A Vichy water perhaps," was his visitor's reply, inclining his head to the waiting attendant. "My digestion is not able to cope with alcohol or strong coffee at any time never mind at such an hour in the morning."

"I am sorry that I suggested this time and place", said Sir George. "But this is a much quieter place than your hotel and I often use it. In fact it was our Officers' Club in the War and hasn't changed much." Then addressing the waiter: "Two Vichy waters, then."

"I am intrigued, Mr Ransome, as to why you wish to meet me and in such an unofficial manner", he continued. "I thought perhaps it was because you had your wife with you."

"No, indeed. I am here at the behest of my newspaper , the Manchester Guardian, to cover these elections", explained the author. "Something of a damp squib, I feel. I think my editor may have expected a repeat of the rather violent events of a few years ago - I covered those. He may well be rather disappointed with the result but I have met a chap called Muggeridge who I am sure would do well with my paper. No, Sir George, I do not take Genia with me on these expeditions so she is at home in Low Ludderburn."

"I know not of it."

"It is our cottage above Lake Windermere. A lovely place, though rather basic. Genia loves the garden and I have established a workroom in the barn which is probably the best I have ever had."

"But you must be rather remote! You have a telephone I presume."

"No, but we have good neighbours and we are developing a sort of signal telegraph. But there is good sailing and fishing to be had."

"Indeed –that I know is of importance to you - but I must confess it is an area of England about which I know little, though I understand my brother's two children had a brief spell there quite recently. Young Richard and Dorothy – a quiet pair – he's very studious. Interested in astronomy."

There was a pause in the conversation as the waiter brought the requested refreshment.

"My family are from Suffolk", Sir George continued. "I commend it to your attention. You can have all sorts of sailing on tidal waters; indeed it seems to be quite common to sail over to Holland -- and there is inland fresh water sailing on the Broads. I think you may like that, as the winds blow more constant across our low country unlike on your northern lakes with their high fells, where the wind can be treacherous, I am told, and a small craft may indeed come to grief on their rocky shores."

"That indeed might well happen."

"And you and your wife – do you keep up your connections with Russia?"

"I can assure you that Genia is not in any way acting for the present Russian regime", was the emphatic answer.

"Nevertheless, your Russian connections continue to exercise HMG", affirmed Sir George.

"Whose interest in me continues to surprise me, as I often remarked. But all that is of no account regarding my latest book."

"Which is about fishing, I believe. I regret that I am an incomplete angler."

" Yes, 'Rod and Line' is about fishing and other things but that is not what I'm talking about. This is a book I shall shortly publish."

".. then it is Politics or sailing?"

"It is based around sailing indeed but it is fiction!"

"I have to confess I am sorry to hear that!"

"Not this modern stuff about sex but a children's story."

"I am amazed!" commented Sir George, meaning it.

"Let me explain how it came about and then you will see why I thought I should have a word with you."

"By all means!"

"The summer before last" began the author. "My dear friend Dora's four children holidayed in the Lake District and we sailed in my two boats – 'Swallow' and 'Mavis' – and we visited islands and coves and explored the hill country around Coniston and Windermere. We fished and played at being pirates – the eldest girl rather enjoyed being a pirate king!. It was a magical time. Then about a year ago they visited me and brought me a present – some Persian slippers – and I knew I had to write a story about them and about sailing in 'Swallow' and having adventures without any grown-ups being involved. Actually, it almost wrote itself."

 Sir George shook his head in disbelief whilst Ransome gushed on - this was not the conversation he had envisaged when agreeing to meet with the distinguished chronicler of events in Russia some ten and more years ago. The rumours of the rise of an Egyptian Communist Party had been rife, so he had – wrongly it would appear - assumed that Ransome was in Egypt in anticipation of some sort of repeat of the Russian events earlier in the century and perhaps, as then, the British Government should be appraised of matters

"So", he said, deciding that this was a trivial matter to be disposed of quickly and politely. "Let me get this right – you have written a book about a friend's children?"
 "No - it's not about them – it's for them."
"But real children in a real location?"
"I have merged the two lakes into one and I did change the family a little so that the eldest is a boy."
"Seems rather unfair!"
"Well not wholly because I put my four in 'Swallow' and I made the eldest of Dora's girls – or someone like her - captain of a rival boat. And I've brought in my tin trunk. I did have problems on my last trip to China – thought it had been stolen at one point. Local rascals thought it was full of money!"

"Mr Ransome, this is a conversation I can see you having with your publishers – but I am at a loss as to why you wished to meet me."

"As well as Dora's family, there were other children around though with a Governess and not so adventurous. They came to us and asked if they might join in – they were not the only ones to do so that summer – and I said they needed their parents' permission. They told us their parents were far away and their Governess had no idea what to do – having heard her fussing about, I was not surprised - but she did have instruction on how to contact the parents by wire. So I ran her down to the telegraph office and showed her how to send a telegram asking for permission to sail and camp. I have kept the reply."

With that, the author reached into a jacket pocket and pulled out a much- folded flimsy sheet and handed it to Sir George.

"I had to do quite a bit of asking, both in the Lakes and through my newspaper, as to who the parents were and had rather given up the chance of meeting them, as they are in the Consular Service. But when I arrived here before Christmas and heard of your name, I established the connection. You spoke earlier of a nephew and niece which clinched the matter for me and so I believe this was sent by your brother."

Sir George looked at the telegram in some considerable surprise.
"Yes -that is certainly from my brother but what does this mean? BETTER DROWNED THAN DUFFERS STOP IF NOT DUFFERS WONT DROWN STOP?"

"That did present a puzzle at the time."

"On reflection I can see my brother in this. One often has to decipher his meaning. And Duffers? yes – I have heard him urge his children not to be duffers – the ultimate sin apparently."

" I'm afraid I rather took to the word and did use it."

"But what did it mean?" asked the now puzzled Sir George.

"Well" explained the author: "As an overseas correspondent, I have sent a few cables in my time but I must confess its message was not immediately apparent. It took Dora's children – the ones who are the are in the book – to decipher it. Apparently their father - like your brother – is often away from his children and does send tricky messages by wire. They interpreted it as meaning 'YES'. So Richard and Dorothy did join us briefly and seemed to have enjoyed themselves despite that rather silly governess having a fit of the vapours when she saw them afloat."

"And all this will be in you book?"

"Not your nephew and niece – though I may draw upon them for future characters – nor your distinguished brother – I have created model parents for my quartet - but I have included the telegram. It may seem out of character for model parents but it is such a remarkable communication, I had to put it in a book! I trust your family will not be angered by this."

"I doubt whether my family will ever come to hear of it. The world of children's fiction is wholly alien to them. So by all means go ahead and publish your book with the telegram in it. I do have to say, I feel it may be just a diversion from your political writing and your prescient political pieces."

" I may not be writing those for much longer. I am tired of it   - tired after China - then this unnecessary trip. I long to be to be back by my lakes and to be in Low Ludderburn in time for the bluebells and the daffodils."

For a moment, Sir George's face took on a more sympathetic air.

"Well, it may be that you feel different when you are back in England"

Sir George now felt that it was high time this rather strange meeting was ended. He reverted to his stern gaze.

"You have an eye for detail Mr Ransome and a great skill in reporting upon that detail," he began. "I am no expert in that field but I cannot think that children wish to read that sort of stuff. Frankly, I do not see you as a children's writer Mr Ransome but I appreciate your good manners in warning me that a most unfortunate communication from my brother will feature in this forthcoming work. I have to say that it all sounds – to me on my first hearing - like a tired man's whimsy. Also – well I'm not sure that a book which recommends that children go boating and camping without adult supervision is something can be commended in any way. But - my view is that this work, which you say you are set on publishing, will be but a flash in the pan and I look forward to you resuming your regular stance as a perceptive political commentator. I wish you, sir, a speedy return to full health and fitness."

With that he stood up. The meeting was over.

As Sir George walked out into the hotel lobby, he reflected that the meeting had indeed been a worthwhile experience – and one he might well relate to others. Most of all - he felt he may well have deflected an important commentator from taking a misguided path into a field in which he was unlikely to succeed. "If I have indeed done that", he said to himself. "It will have been a GOOD MORNING."

AUTHOR'S POSTSCRIPT

The foregoing is written purely in homage to the memory of a writer whose works much affected my childhood and I hope I have not offended the members of TARS, The Arthur Ransome Society [www.arthur-ransome.org.uk], whose knowledge of the life and works of the remarkable writer is so much deeper than my own.

In researching this tale, I have been indebted to:
The Last Englishman: the Double Life of Arthur Ransome, Roland Chambers; [Faber and Faber 2009], *The World of Arthur Ransome*, Christina Hardyment; [Frances Lincoln 2012] also her *Arthur Ransome and Capt. Flint's Trunk* [Jonathan Cape 1984] together with the background of reading all 12 books in the *Swallows and Amazons* series by the age of twelve and the recent acquisition of TARS publications. I should acknowledge also that Karen Babayan has rather beaten me into this field with *Swallows and Armenians* [Wild Pansy Press 2019].

Swallows and Amazons and the sequel *Swallowdale* are on my shelves and I have returned to them several times for, as we all know, this particular Sir George was - like Rick in Casablanca – "misinformed". So I raise a metaphorical glass to TARS with their toast "Swallows and Amazons For Ever!".

JUNE 2015

"Good morning, Sir George."

Sir George Calderdale, puffing a little, having rushed up the steps to gain the main level of the Lord's Pavilion and then again up the rather steep staircase to the Bowlers' Bar, and with a worrying recurrence of that stab behind the breastbone- a sign of his undoubted advancing years – peered around the busy little bar in search of the caller.

"Sir George – we're over here."

The call from the familiar voice came again and he located his young fellow cricket fanatic and family lawyer, Krishnan, with the young female companion he expected to meet, seated at a corner table by a window which looked out over the balcony to the deserted playing area on this depressingly wet June Sunday morning. The baronet gave a wave of acknowledgement and wended his way through the throng who, driven in by the rain, had started their lunchtime imbibing earlier than perhaps they had anticipated.

 The genial clientele on this Sunday was different from a weekday, when it would consist almost entirely of those gentlemen who could find the time to watch County Cricket. There were the usual well-tailored suits but those were outnumbered by top-of -the range blazers, accompanied a variety of club ties, Middlesex, MCC and a few representing the visitors, Hampshire County Cricket Club. Also today, the scene was enlivened with a sprinkling of ladies, perhaps enjoying the chance of a good lunch and the possibility of mingling with important people. It was a clientele not in any way surprised to overhear that a baronet was in their company.

"Good to see you Krishnan," said Sir George, taking off his wet mac and rather casually, throwing it to one side. It was a gesture of some irritation , for Sir George -financier, business tycoon, property magnate as the Press variously described him – did not like to have his plans messed up. He slowly eased his considerable bulk into the chair which had - with some difficulty - been saved for him. In an indication of his irritability, he ignored the lady at the table and addressed himself solely to Krishnan.

"Sorry, I'm late – as I texted, the trains are all up the chute on a Sunday." He half arose and looked through the window to the giant electronic scoreboard only to see that it was displaying the rather obvious information that rain had stopped play.

"Has there been any play?" he asked.

"We got a start", was the reply from the younger man. "Middlesex won the toss and we inserted them. The track was doing a bit and we got both openers for not a lot -one for Murts, one for Toby – both caught by Simmo –."

"Gee!" came the comment with an American tinge to it from the – so far ignored - young lady. "What ARE you guys talking about?"

"Heavens" said Krishnan. "How rude of me! Sir George this is Jenny who - as I said - has done a terrific job and has got something for us."

On the introductions, Sir George looked at Jenny, seeing someone, who on first sight, looked like being more used to jeans and a sweater than her rather ill-fitting, charity shop sourced trouser suit and whose pallid countenance suggested she was more used to being in amongst dusty old papers than out in the fresh air at a sporting venue.

To Jenny, Sir George had become an almost mythical person in the six months she had been working on his ancestry but she decided he looked much as she expected on first hearing about him.

That had occurred when Val, a colleague at the museum, and technically her line manager, asked her to join her husband, Krishnan, and herself for a drink after work one day in the previous autumn. Jenny was rather surprised, as Oxford educated Val had always seemed a little stand-offish, but it turned out that this was not entirely a social occasion. They had a mission for her.

Krishnan had introduced himself: "*I am the family solicitor for a stubborn old Yorkshire chap called Sir George Calderwood who is proving to be a bit of a problem for his family. They own an enormous chain of businesses- they've been going since the 19th century -and he's the Chairman and Managing Director and principal shareholder and he's just gone AWOL while he traces his family right back to goodness knows where. He has got it into his head that somewhere there was a branch of his family who were given land by the king and he cannot find this king though he has gone back centuries.*"
"*The fourteenth no less!*" interjected his wife.
"*He is obsessed, in fact last year it absorbed all his time - totally neglected the business - and even his cricket's taken a back seat. The old beggar just won't resign and let his perfectly capable family run the show. His doctor is worried about him too. If something isn't done the business is going to collapse.*"
Jenny was puzzled. "*So why am I here?*"

"We have tried to get him to employ Family History Consultants – he can certainly afford them! – but he says they're all posh southern gits and he wouldn't give them the time of day."

"So that rather leaves me out" laughed Val.

Krishnan continued: *"So we thought of you. Val tells me you are the best medievalist she has ever encountered even though you are actually from the United States."*

Somewhat astonished at this compliment, Jenny trotted out her well – rehearsed life story.

"I was born in Connecticut but my mother was English. You see - my paw was in the USAAF and he was at a place called Burtonwood -it's up north near a place called Warrington in your Chess -shire county- and he met my maw and they got married and came stateside - she couldn't wait to leave Warrington I've been there - I can see why. So I have a British passport – came here as student- stayed ever since so I'm sort of English now - though I don't understand your cricket."

"You are not alone there!" affirmed Val.

"So I just kinda took naturally to British history - we have nothing like that back in the states – and I got into medieval Latin, Anglo- Saxon, Norman French – and - I just love it!"

Krishnan expounded further. *"We hope you can use your amazing skill to prove once and for all that, sometime, somewhere a king gave Sir George's ancestor – and he thinks it was in Northumberland not Yorkshire – a grant of land. When we've proved that conclusively, we can get the old boy to re-connect and rescue the business before it collapses and I reckon we've got about six months. So we need you to give your time well into next year."*

Jenny looked at Val: *"But what about the Museum?"*

"We've thought about that," replied Val, *" and we have a solution. The Museum will give you study leave – largely because they think there's a book in all this, So this could be good for them and good for your career. Sorry to spring all this on you."*

"What period exactly are we looking at?"

"Sir George has gone all the way back to the fourteenth century – in great detail but has drawn a blank. So we need to look at earlier periods" replied Val. *"I've actually had a look myself – at his wife's request and without him knowing. As you know Jenny, this is not my period and other than checking his research – which looks very thorough - I could get nowhere. There was no sign of any royal grant."*

"Are we doing this in secret?" Jenny was surprised.

"Let us say we are doing this as a surprise birthday present."

"Ok I can go along with that but you will have to give me all the reference points."

"I have done that already – it's in my room at the Museum and you could pick it up tomorrow," replied Val. *" I think it has got all the relative names and places. So you would start by looking at the early thirteen- hundreds or thereabouts – your period I think."*

"Very much so – but if this is north England you are talking about then that was a very troubled time – there were wars with Scottish people. – and I know that records can be difficult to trace."

"But you will help?"

"Try and stop me!"

Though now able to report success, she did not really know where to start and when Krishnan departed to get drinks at the bar, was pleased when Sir George spotted her discomfiture and began to put her at ease:

"This is your first visit to Lords, I understand" he began.

"Yessir. I'm a nutmegger."

As a cricketing person, the word "nutmeg" meant something rather painful to Sir George so he looked puzzled.

"I 'm from Hartford, Connecticut, USA" explained Jenny. "But putting down roots here, I'm getting married to a UK citizen."

"And I live in Hertfordshire, England" came the reply. "But I don't want to. Forced to move south by the wife when we moved my company's headquarters out of Yorkshire. I was against it but at least I can get to the cricket here."

"This is sure some place. I thought this would be like your House of Lords but it's a sort of baseball park named after a guy called Thomas Lord – is that right"

"Dead right, lass – A Yorkshireman like me."

"Everybody's so well dressed! In that long room with the pictures, everybody talks in whispers! And this is the first of FOUR days!"

Sir George was saved the near impossible task of explaining cricket in general and County Cricket in particular to an American by the return of Krishnan with the drinks.

"I've got your usual Sir George", he began then sat down. "You know we have been worried about your obsessing with family history and the granting of land long ago. Well your worries are over – Jenny – tell him."

"I have not brought the papers but I am one hundred percent certain you are correct in asserting a king gave land to your ancestor," proclaimed the American.

 "I knew all along!" Sir George cried in glee.

"But you had been looking in the wrong place. You see the king who gave that land was the king in Scotland."

"Scotland!"

"Your Northumberland -shire county – at that time was – for all practical purposes- ruled by Scotland! I went to Edinburgh city and checked. I had not previously been there – my partner from Sussex county was with me – and neither of us had been there. I had no idea about the place –London folks kidded me we would have to live on oats and whisky – and everyone was mean and would hate us. And I kinda thought by now it would be a county like your Yorkshire – but -boy was I wrong!   - and did they not tell me! - a Connecticut Yankee putting her big foot in it! But Edinburgh was just dandy – historic and scenic and really good restaurants. Everyone was really helpful and I found out everything I needed and my partner and I had a great time!"
"Good to hear" said Krishnan.
Jenny continued gleefully. "And I can absolutely guarantee an ancestor of Sir George received a gift of land in1326!"

"I can't tell you what this means to me"" Sir George paused for a moment making little clicking noises with his tongue against his front teeth. " Let me pay for you and your bloke on your honeymoon .. we own a chain of hotels .."
"Actually Sir George, my partner is another woman."
"Ee heck is that legal now!"
"Since March of last year to be exact Sir George" Krishnan pointed out gently.
"I've got so out of touch .. ee -I'm so sorry lass .. whatever must you be thinking of me. Ne'er mind ... Krishnan, is it legal in Scotland too?"
"Since last December! And Jenny - with my wife – is going to write a book about your ancestry – if that is all right with you."
Sir George had reached one of the sudden decisions for which he was famous. "Today – suddenly everything is right. It occurs to me -right here and now - I've had enough of all

this Ancestry business – you can have all my papers wi'
pleasure lass."

"A lot of people might be pleased to hear that" said Krishnan
pointedly but Sir George had more.

"It's taken this young lass to make me see I've let things slip
and I'm getting on. It's about time I retired and let the next
generation carry on! Krishnan, there will be things to do."

" Two things immediately -" the lawyer replied with obvious
relief in his tone, " – arrange for all those papers to get to
Jenny and right now – head for lunch – I think the rain has
eased."

As the trio walked down to the Grace Gates and the Tavern,
the weather showing signs of improvement, Sir George,
conscious of having made major lifestyle decisions, felt an
unaccustomed spring in his stride. "By heck " he announced
to nobody in particular, "-I've had a GOOD MORNING."

AUTHOR'S POSTSCRIPT

For the facts behind this fiction I have drawn on over thirty
years' happy membership of Middlesex County Cricket
Club and am obliged to my copy of their Handbook for 2015
and *Wars Of The Bruces* Colm McNamee [Tuckwell 1997]
For cricket fans the match details were:
Hampshire 178 & 227 MCCC 330 and 77-1. Middlesex won
by 9 wickets. In the 2015 Season MCCC won 7 out of 16
and finished second [well behind] Yorkshire
My apologies to all my family and my quizzing and sporting
friends in the thriving Borough of Warrington in Chess-
shire county.

Here we leave this assortment of entirely fictional men called "Sir George" but we are not leaving Lord's Cricket Ground as Marion Pitman takes us back in time.

THE

CASE OF THE

MISSING WICKET KEEPER

by Marion Pitman

EDITORIAL NOTE

Given that reports of events on a cricket field in the first decade of the 20th century which have not been recorded in a scorebook have to be considered anecdotal evidence, the cricketing incident and comments by Dr W G Grace are presented here as actual occurrences, having been recorded in Sir Arthur Conan Doyle's 1924 autobiography *Memories and Adventures* and duly quoted in Chap. 31 of Simon Rae's magisterial *W. G. Grace* [Faber & Faber 1998].

Both Donald and Marion would like to express their appreciation of the current high standard of wicketkeeping in Women's Cricket.

THE CASE
OF THE MISSING WICKETKEEPER

"Your friend Doyle's trousers appear to be on fire," observed Holmes. "No doubt the ball which struck his thigh has ignited a box of vestas incautiously placed in a pocket."

Holmes's deduction was as usual precisely accurate. The batsman was at that moment hauling the offending box out of his flannels to hurl it on to the pitch and stamp out the flames. We were at Lord's, watching Dr. Doyle play for MCC against Kent, and a small diversion had just been caused by this incendiary incident. Holmes was not enthralled by the game – apart from boxing and fencing, sport held little appeal for him, and the brief diversion seemed to cheer him up. You will of course know Dr Doyle – I should now say Sir Arthur, of course - as the man who presents my accounts of my friend's cases to a long-suffering public. He had prevailed upon us to come to the match so that he might consult Holmes about a problem, and Holmes had reluctantly agreed, having just finished solving the mystery of the coastguard's parrot, and needing therefore a fresh problem to work upon. The match was early in the season, and it was a very wet summer as you may remember, so we were sitting muffled in overcoats, which is not the best way to watch cricket. We had missed the first day, as Holmes had been busy in the morning, and in fact play had not been possible until well after lunch, but we had arrived in good time for the second day, and Doyle had thanked us and expressed his intention of buying us dinner after close of play.

Holmes was watching the spectators as much as the players, and as they came off at the end of the day, he nudged me and said, "Do you see that girl in the blue hat and coat, three rows back in the next stand? Do you recognise her?"

"I can't say I do," I replied. "Do you know her?"

"Not at all; but she came in about half an hour ago, and she has been fixedly watching Dr Doyle, and occasionally glancing over at us. I would be willing to bet a small sum that she is connected to this problem we are to investigate."

Once again Holmes's deduction was correct; as we waited for Doyle at the door of the pavilion, we saw the girl in blue also waiting, and when the doctor came out he greeted her, then introduced us:

"Alice, this is Dr. Watson, and Mr Sherlock Holmes. Gentlemen, Miss Alice Shaw, whom I am hoping we shall be able to help."

We all expressed gratification at the meeting, and Doyle took us to a quiet restaurant in St John's Wood, not far from the ground. Presently he began,

"Miss Shaw is engaged to be married to young Richard Knights, who plays for my old team in Norwood, and has some hopes of playing for his county. A first-class wicketkeeper, and a very decent bat. Alice, would you explain to Mr Holmes the events of the last two weeks?"

Miss Shaw blushed a little and fiddled with her cutlery, then said, "Mr Holmes, I am very much afraid something has happened to Richard. Two weeks ago we had dinner together, and then went to a respectable hotel and had a glass of wine. He walked me home, and he said he would see me the next day – he is a clerk in an office near where I work as a typist, and we generally meet after work and spend some time together. The next day he didn't appear, and I was a little concerned; I sent him a note. I heard nothing the next day either; the day after that I asked a colleague of mine to call at Richard's office, and find out if he were unwell. My colleague told me that they had had a note from Richard giving in his notice, and they had not seen him since the day I saw him last.

"In the end I went round to his lodgings; his landlady had not seen him since then either and said he had taken his things and left her a week's rent in lieu of notice.

"Mr Holmes, there must be something wrong. Even if – as someone suggested – he had run into debt and decided to levant, he would have got in touch with me somehow. We had been talking about fixing the date of our wedding. I can't believe he would just leave me without a word."

There was something of an embarrassed silence when she had finished; I'm afraid I was thinking, and I suspected the other two were also, that young Mr Knights had clearly repented of his engagement and had taken a rather drastic and dishonourable way out of it.

However, Doyle clearly believed that there was more to it. I looked at Holmes, who was frowning into his glass of wine. Presently he said,

"Very distressing for you, Miss Shaw. It is all too easy for a man to disappear in London. However, I have cracked harder cases. Firstly, then, does Mr Knights have any close family who might know of his whereabouts?"

"I'm sure he hasn't left of his own accord, Mr Holmes. To the best of my knowledge he has no family. He told me that he is an only child, and his parents are dead; he didn't want to talk about his childhood, and I thought it must hold unhappy memories. He has never mentioned any relatives or close friends. He is friendly with some of the other clerks in his office, but they're not close."

"Has he ever mentioned where he lived before he came to London? If he has no friends or family at all nearby, it suggests his origins lie elsewhere."

"As I say, he doesn't like to talk about his past, but two or three times he has mentioned Wickham, in Hampshire, and I wondered if that might be his family home. I have never pursued the matter, though – I wouldn't want to distress him."

"How long have you known him?"

"Close on two years. We met by chance, at a tea dance at St Andrew's. We have been engaged for six months."

"St. Andrew's – are you regular churchgoers?"

"I go to St. Luke's, which is near where I live, but I don't think Richard goes to church at all, he's never mentioned it."

"What else can you tell me? Have you made any plans, for example about where you will live when you marry?"

"No. Richard says he doesn't care to plan too far ahead, you never know what may happen."

"And what about your family? What do they think of the young man?"

"My father is dead, Mr Holmes. My mother lives with my brother and his wife in Manchester. I've tried to persuade Richard to come up and visit them, but he says there'll be plenty of time when we've fixed a date for the wedding."

"Does he have any hobbies which engage his attention?"

"As Sir Arthur says, he plays cricket, and in winter he goes running. He dances, though not very well." She smiled.

Sir Arthur put in, "I have made enquiries at the cricket club and the harriers – none of the men there knows Knights well, they all say he was frank and friendly in manner, but never spoke of his home or family. They were all astonished to hear of his disappearance."

Holmes continued, "Well then, it remains only to ask you for the address of Mr Knights' lodgings and his place of work, and a description of his appearance."

Miss Shaw gave the addresses, and said, "He's a very good-looking – sorry, that's not helpful. He's not very tall, not much taller than me, and slightly built. Brown hair, brown eyes, no moustache - I have a photograph ..." She hunted in her capacious handbag, and produced a leather pocket book, from which she took three photographs – one was a large group on an outing, in which it was difficult to distinguish anyone; one was a family group of Miss Shaw as a child with her parents and brother; the third was a slightly overexposed snapshot of a young man in a blazer and a straw hat: he had a roundish face, very fair skinned and clean-shaven, and a cheerful, light-hearted look about him – boyish, and much like hundreds of other young men. Holmes studied it carefully. Miss Shaw said, "It's the only picture I have of him..."

The detective smiled and handed it back. "I have a good memory for faces," he said. "Miss Shaw, I can promise nothing, but I will do what I can."

"Will it ... be very expensive?" she asked nervously.

Doyle made a faintly protesting noise, and Holmes said, "I assure you it will not be more than you can afford."

She smiled, and the talk moved to the day's play, and, inevitably, to the vesta incident, and Dr W G Grace's comment – "Couldn't get you out - had to set you on fire!"

As Holmes and I strolled back to Baker Street, he said, "Well, Watson, this may be nothing at all, but it has one or two promising angles. Do you care to accompany me tomorrow on a visit to Mr Knights' office and lodging?"

"I have my rounds in the morning," I said, "but in the afternoon I am at your disposal."

"Excellent! I will call for you at two."

            #   #
                              #

The following afternoon saw Holmes and myself
taking a hansom to the suburb of Lower Norwood – familiar
to us both from the affair of Jonas Oldacre. On the way
Holmes told me of his morning's inquiries at Knights' place
of work, an accountancy business.

"They speak very highly of him, and are sorry to lose
him, but his sudden departure seems to have been a surprise
to everyone. One young fellow rather hinted that Knights was
unhappy about his engagement but couldn't suggest why he
should bolt like this. He seems to have been well regarded
by his employers, and popular with the other clerks. I
wondered if there might be any other young woman in his
life, but there is no evidence of it. There are two female
typists employed in the office, but one is about fifty years of
age, and the other is engaged to be married in two weeks'
time. If I am to find a clue, I think it will have to be with the
landlady we are about to meet, Mrs Fairbrother."

Mrs Fairbrother was a tall, well-built woman of forty or
so, with dark hair and a brisk manner. When she learned
our errand, she began at once to exclaim and lament – "The
nicest young man you could wish to meet, Mr Holmes.
Always polite, no drinking or smoking, always on time with
the rent. I can't think what could have made him run off like
this. Never any trouble with women, no-one for him but Miss
Shaw, bless her, such a sweet thing as she is. You could have
knocked me down with a feather. So you think something's
happened to him? That's her idea, I know, and I own I can
hardly believe he'd just leave her flat like this. Will you have
a cup of tea?"

Without waiting for our acceptance she put the kettle
on, and Holmes took advantage of the brief pause to ask, "I
was wondering if you knew of any family or close friends Mr
Knights   has,   who   might   know   something   of   his

whereabouts?"

"Well, no, I don't. He always said he was an orphan and had no friends in London. I never heard of his having no family, except for his sister."

"His sister!" I exclaimed, and the good woman went on.

"It was his sister who engaged the room for him. She came in to see it, and explained it was for her brother, who was arriving on a very late train from the country, and needed somewhere to stay that night – she said he had lost his job suddenly, and got a new one in London, and had to start right away. She said if I'd let her have the key, she'd let him in when he arrived. Well, I wasn't quite happy, but she paid me a month's rent in advance, and I thought, well, I can keep an eye on them, and after all a month's rent is a month's rent.

"So I gave her the key and left her with his trunk – he'd sent his trunk on ahead – and I went to bed about midnight; and in the morning there Mr Knights was down at breakfast, and everything quite right about him – until this."

She paused to pour the tea, and Holmes said, "Did he send or receive any letters, Mrs Fairbrother?"

"Well, not to say letters. I never saw him with anything for the post, but of course he could do that from the office, couldn't he? As to receiving, nothing but the usual things, a bill now and then, a letter from his bank now and then – he was saving up for his wedding – and of course a note now and then from Miss Shaw. I never noticed anything else."

"I don't suppose you know who he banked with, Mrs Fairbrother?"

"Well, as a matter of fact, it was Boult's, in Cheapside. I just happened to see the name once, on the envelope."

Holmes made a note, and said, "Did you observe anything unusual about Mr Knights?"

"Nothing at all. He was a very ordinary young man, but most obliging. The only thing that ever seemed odd, the day after he came there was quite an unpleasant smell in the room. But it went away."

"What kind of smell?"

"A bit like burning, very bitter."

"As if he had been burning papers?"

"Oh no, nothing like that."

"Can you describe his sister for me?"

The landlady frowned; "Well, I don't know. She was very ordinary – not very short or tall, not very fat or thin. I think she had fairish hair. And her eyes were sensitive - she wore tinted spectacles. But I couldn't say I'd know her again, to be honest."

"Thank you so much, Mrs Fairbrother. Watson, if you've finished your tea, we'll leave this good lady to get on with her work." And in a tide of speculation and lamenting Mrs Fairbrother saw us to the door.

Holmes was silent on the return journey, a sign that his mind was working on the recent information. He dropped me outside my surgery, and said, "I suppose I can't persuade you to take a few days off, Watson?"

"I'm afraid not for a day or two, Holmes. I am engaged to visit friends tomorrow, and don't like to cry off, and I have a good many appointments on Monday."

"Very well. I may go down to Hampshire – I will let you know when I return."

It was in fact on the fourth day, which was the Wednesday, that on rising I received a note from Holmes, delivered by hand at 6 a.m., that read, "The game's afoot – come to breakfast." Smiling at this echo of old days, I asked my neighbour if he would take my appointments and went round to Baker Street.

The coffee, the eggs and bacon were as good as ever. As we ate, Holmes said, "I'm hoping you'll accompany me out to Wimbledon, Watson. I think I may have tracked down our quarry."

"Quick work, Holmes. So is Mr Knights alive and well, then? Or are we on the track of murder?"

"Well – yes and no. Forgive me – I may be quite wrong, and I would prefer to verify my deductions before going into more detail."

"Well, did he disappear willingly, or was he abducted?"

"Oh, entirely willingly. Marmalade?"

It was never any use to press Holmes for a deduction he was not ready to disclose, so I focussed on the excellent breakfast, and he discoursed on medieval church music, until I drained the last of my coffee, and we went out to take a cab to Wimbledon.

On the journey he assuaged some of my curiosity – "Well, Watson, I have been active since I saw you. My first visit was to Boult's bank. Of course the bank was not going to reveal any information about a client to a mere consulting detective, but I contrived to get an interview with the manager and deduced that Mr Knights' account was still with them and in a healthy condition, and that they had no worries about him. I also gathered from an incautious aside that he was still residing somewhere in the London area.

"I then went down to Wickham, in Hampshire. From talk with local people, I have got on the track of a Miss Rowena Templar."

"Yes? Is she concerned in the business?"

"From what I can gather, she physically resembles the lady who called on Mrs Fairbrother."

"Knights' sister?"

"Miss Templar appears to have no brother, however. She left her family home about two years ago and has not been seen since. She quarrelled with her parents – her father is a well-to-do merchant – over the question of marriage. She is now five and twenty years of age, and her father was urging her to marry a successful young lawyer who had been courting her for a couple of years. Miss Templar is a very independent-spirited and energetic young woman, and prefers target-shooting, tennis and cricket to more feminine pursuits. She showed no interest in marrying, rousing her father's anger; one morning the household arose to find she had decamped in the night, and they have heard nothing from her since then."

"Have they looked for her? Do you think she and Knights went off together? Perhaps they met through an interest in sport... But what has become of them both?"

"As to that, I am not yet certain. But the other thing I discovered is that an older woman, who had been governess to Miss Templar and was still living in the house as a paid companion of some kind, left about six months ago, having come into a small inheritance from an aunt, and is rumoured to be living in Wimbledon. I have had enquiries made in Wimbledon and think I have found her."

"So you think – this companion may know what happened to Miss Templar, and she may lead us to young Knights?"

Holmes laughed a little as I spoke, and said, "Something of the kind. By the way, I also ascertained that not long before she left home, Miss Templar also inherited quite a sum of money, from her grandmother. So she had the wherewithal to pay for good lodgings and support herself while she looked about for employment."

"But I cannot see how finding this girl can lead us to the young man. You have established no real connection between them, except that she resembles the rather inadequate description of Mrs Fairbrother's visitor."

"True. But recall the tinted spectacles, which suggest a disguise. Consider that Miss Shaw never heard young Knights mention a sister. Consider the appearance of

Knights in the photograph, and the description of Miss Templar's character. What conclusion do you draw from all that?"

"Only that someone may have pretended to be Knights' sister, in order to engage the room, so presumably something prevented him from engaging it himself – why was he only able to arrive at Mrs Fairbrother's in the middle of the night? And where has Miss Templar been in the meantime? Has she been in Wimbledon all the time, do you think?"

"Not all the time. But I hope to find her there now."

"And Knights? Where is he?"

"I have some hope we may find him in Wimbledon too. But to say any more would be to speculate, a thing I deplore, as you know, Watson. How extensive is your knowledge of the French Romantic poets?"

My knowledge was not extensive, but Holmes extended it considerably during the rest of our journey.

In Wimbledon, we drew up at a small semi-detached house with the name "Belleville". Holmes knocked briskly on the green painted door, which was presently opened by a woman of fifty or so with a pleasantly rounded figure and her hair in a bun; her dark brown dress was modest but of good quality.

"Miss Partridge?" said Holmes, "I am looking for Miss Rowena Templar. May we come in?"

Miss Partridge hesitated, then said, "May I ask what is your business with Miss Templar
?"

Holmes produced a card – "My name is Sherlock Holmes; I am a consulting detective; I have been trying to locate Miss Templar."

The woman paled as she looked at the card. "What makes you think," she said at last, "that Miss Templar is here?"

"She may not be, but I think you know where she is. I have also been asked to locate a Mr Richard Knights, whom you may or may not know."

Her eyes widened –I thought the name had startled her. She bit her lip, and said,

"You had better come in. Please wait in the parlour – I will be down shortly."

We were shown into a shabby and comfortable front parlour, and our hostess mounted the stairs. I sat in a welcoming if worn armchair, and Holmes paced the floor, his eye alternately on the door and the window. He said,

"I hope our bird does not decide to fly. There is the back door, of course, but escaping over the garden wall might provide a challenge. Ah! Someone is coming down."

He had the door of the room open, and Mrs Partridge appeared at the foot of the stairs, followed by a shortish young man with brown hair and a city suit.

The woman said, "Mr Knights will see you," and turned towards the back of the house; the young man came towards us –

"Mr Sherlock Holmes," he said, extending his hand, "I had no idea I was such an important person as to warrant the exercise of your talents. And the good Dr Watson too -" I rose as he came into the room – "I won't ask how you found me, since you are Sherlock Holmes – but what do you want with me? I haven't broken the law, so far as I know. So how can I help you?"

We all sat down, and Holmes said, "No law, no, but certain considerations of good behaviour. I won't ask why you left Miss Shaw, but why ever did you court her in the first place – Miss Templar?"

I sat up with a jerk, and the young man turned very pale, so much that I feared he might faint. He took a deep breath, however, and said, "I beg your pardon?"

"It is the obvious solution," said Holmes, "it fits all the facts. The mysterious sister, the young man arriving at his lodgings at dead of night, and then a young woman who closely resembles him, and also plays cricket, and has disappeared – the likelihood that there is in fact only one person involved is high. It would not, of course, be difficult to prove, but I cannot detain you, I admit."

The supposed Richard Knights breathed heavily for a while, then said, "How did you find Mrs Partridge?"

"You mentioned Wickham two or three times to Miss Shaw. She is a young woman in love with a man of mysterious antecedents, she remembers every unexplained reference. Once I visited Wickham I quickly heard of the disappearing Miss Templar, who is of course still a lively subject of gossip and conjecture, and thereafter the fairly recent departure of Miss Partridge soon came into the conversation. Miss Partridge had taken no great pains to cover her trail, but I imagine you thought no-one would connect Miss Templar with Mr Richard Knights. "

"Well, the job I undertook is completed: I have ascertained that Mr Richard Knights is alive and well and free to come and go. Should I report back to that effect to Miss Shaw? Or can you give me a good reason why I should not?"

Knights leaned back in his chair for some time, and said at last, "Would you care for a drink, Mr Holmes? Doctor? Miss Partridge keeps quite a decent whisky, as well as sherry and gin."

Holmes laughed. "Well," he said, "I will accept a small whisky and soda – Watson?"

I agreed, and Knights poured three drinks at a mahogany sideboard and brought them to us. He resumed his seat, and said,

"It never crossed my mind that Alice would set a detective on my trail, let alone Sherlock Holmes. Shall I begin at the beginning? It's the usual thing.

"When I was a child, I always liked playing boys' games, doing boys' things – no good at needlework or embroidery, or genteel watercolour painting. When you're a child it's all right, people smile and shake their heads, but when you grow up and you still want to shoot and fish, play cricket and run about generally, it's not allowed. Father got so angry when I wouldn't marry poor Mr. Walters – a decent enough fellow, but a dreadful shot, and a shockingly inept batsman – that I made up my mind to leave home. I had my grandmother's money, and I could set up on my own – women do that sort of thing nowadays, it wouldn't be as utterly shocking as it would have in been in Grandmother's day. But then I thought, yes, but it would be even easier if I were a man. And it would be much easier to get a job if I were a man. The fact is that a man can get a job twice as easily as a woman and get paid more for it too. I had studied bookkeeping, because Father thinks a woman should be able to keep the household accounts and help her husband in his business! So I decided to go to London and look about for a situation.

"Of course I left Wickham as a woman; I put up at a railway hotel for a few nights in London and studied the advertisements in the papers for situations and lodgings. I thought that it would be a good idea to live a little way out of the city, then people wouldn't expect to visit me at home and get too friendly. I was anxious to disappear completely as Miss Templar before my new personality appeared – I rather enjoyed choosing the name – did you appreciate that, Mr Holmes?"

"I did indeed – Knights Templar – though I fear Watson missed the joke."

Sometimes Holmes can be unnecessarily irritating. I took a pull at my whisky and soda.

"I emptied and closed Miss Templar's bank account;

I packed my trunk and took all my things to Mrs Fairbrother's, engaged the room on behalf of my brother, and sat in it until the house was quiet. Then I set about transforming myself. I cut my hair short – I got it cut properly at a barber's next day – and burned the hair in the fireplace. It smelt horrible. Then I unpacked the suit of men's clothes I had bought in town, and Mr Richard Knights got a few hours' sleep and came down to breakfast.

"Oh, and I'd got a pair of tinted spectacles for my sister – a family resemblance is one thing, but I thought I'd better not risk it too far.

"I managed to get an office boy's job at Spicer's and got promoted within the year – I was proud of that – and set about to establish my new identity. I opened an account at Boult's, put some of Grandmother's money in it, though not all, and settled down to enjoy myself. I joined a cricket club – I'm a pretty good wicketkeeper, Doctor, and a passable bat – and led the life of a perfectly ordinary young man.

"Then I met Alice. She's a lovely girl, Mr Holmes – I'm very fond of her. She took to me, and I thought having a young woman would help my disguise, in case anyone got on my track. But – she's very strong minded, in a sort of timid way. After a year or so, I found she was talking about getting married. I really don't remember proposing at all, but I somehow found I had bought her a ring, and we were engaged. It bothered me considerably, but after all, engaged just means walking in the park, and kissing a bit. I'd rather kiss Alice than poor Walters. Alice's family were all miles away, and I said mine were dead. It didn't seem a problem.

"After a bit, though, she kept on about setting a date for the wedding, and I realised I was in some difficulty. I couldn't quite bring myself just to say I'd changed my mind – and she might bring an action for breach of promise, which would have been very awkward. I'm afraid I panicked and ran away. You seem to have followed all that pretty well. Miss Partridge was the only person from home I'd kept in touch with, and I knew she'd got this place in Wimbledon. I asked her to take me in – she's as close as an oyster is Partridge, she wouldn't talk about it – and it would give me a breathing space. I'd left Mrs Fairbrother a week's rent over what was owing, so she'd have no reason to chase me. Spicer's would be annoyed, but I didn't think they'd bother too much. I should have known Alice wouldn't let it go easily."

"She thought you had been abducted or made away with."

"Yes, I see. I should have sent her a note or something. Well – you see – the thing is, so long as I'm in England I shall worry that someone might recognise me. I've made up my mind I shall go to Australia. There's a lot of space there, and not half so many people. They've given women the vote, too. I'm trying to persuade Partridge to come with me. So, Mr Holmes, could you hold off telling Alice the truth for a few weeks? I suppose she'll hate me, but I can't marry her, can I? I don't think I'm cut out for marriage, to tell the truth. And frankly I'm too much of a coward to tell her myself."

"It would be the better course," said Holmes. "but I cannot force you. It would be a kindness, though, to let her know you are alive and well. May I tell her that?"

"I'll tell you what, if you'll keep silence for a while, I'll write Alice a farewell letter. Thank you, Mr Holmes. I swear I never thought to warrant the attention of the world's greatest detective – I feel positively flattered!"

Holmes laughed shortly. "Well, thank you for the drink – Mr Knights, since that is who you are at the moment. And thank Miss Partridge, since I surmise it is her whisky. If you can tell us where to find a cab, we will leave you to make your preparations for your new life in the antipodes."

#   #
#

Holmes remained dissatisfied – he had solved the case, and his reasoning was triumphantly accurate as usual, but he had nothing to tell his client. A few days later, however, I was with him in the Baker Street flat after dinner, when a tap on the door heralded Sir Arthur and Miss Shaw.

Miss Shaw accepted a seat, and said, "Mr Holmes, I am so grateful to you and to Sir Arthur. Richard is safe and well – he is not coming back, but he has written me a letter that has quite set my mind at rest as to his welfare." She proffered a couple of sheets of writing paper, and Holmes took them and read aloud:

"My Dear Alice, though I suppose I should not say that, as you are no longer my dear.

I have first of all to tell you how sorry I am for worrying you, and then how sorry I am that we cannot be married. But you will find a much better man than I, and will be very happy, I'm sure.

"I had a terrible shock the other day and acted quite madly. But I must do what I must do, and I could not see you again for fear it should undermine my resolve.

"I told you I had no family, but that was not true. I have a brother, who long ago went to Canada. We had quite lost touch, but I have now heard from him for the first time in many years. He is gravely ill and in trouble, and there is no-one for him to turn to except me. I am taking a passage to Halifax; I have no idea when or indeed if I shall return. It would therefore be out of the question to ask you to wait for me. I am not half good enough for you anyway. I can only ask you not to think too harshly of me and hope that you find someone who comes close to deserving you. I will always count myself honoured to have known you, and remain,
Yours very faithfully
Richard Knights

P.S. Mr Sherlock Holmes has tracked me down and told me of your anxiety. I apologize again for causing you concern. I have asked Mr Holmes to wait until I have left the country before reporting to you. Please forgive him for indulging me."

Holmes returned the missive without comment.

Miss Shaw said, "I should be angry with you, Mr Holmes, but I understand his determination, and I thank you."

"It has been an interesting case, Miss Shaw. I am sorry I cannot restore your fiancé, but at least now you need not fear he has come to harm. I hope you will in time recover from your disappointment."

"Oh, Mr Holmes, to know that he has sacrificed himself in a noble cause is more than enough recompense. I wish that I could have gone with him – but I fear I am not cut out for the pioneering life. I feel privileged to have known him. I cannot thank you enough."

She and Sir Arthur stood to take their leave, and Dr. Doyle said, "A noble undertaking, Watson, and a great loss to the noble game. Possibly the best wicketkeeper I've ever seen – remarkably quick, very safe pair of hands, and a good eye. A great loss – but of course there are many things more important than cricket! A fine young man."

He smiled, and shook hands, and they left, not without Miss Shaw thanking Holmes several more times. As the door closed, my friend poured himself a glass of brandy.

"Upon my word, Watson, I was afraid she was going to embrace me. I am glad she has not vowed to be true to him forever – you recall the sad case of Miss Mary

Sutherland – or to follow him to Canada, since that's not where he is going.

"Young Knights has a way with words, though, hasn't he – a most moving and inventive epistle. I shall look out for the next great romantic novelist to come from Australia."

I laughed, then frowned – "I'm more worried about the next visit of our doughty Antipodean cricketing opponents," I said, "if he is as good a 'keeper as Sir Arthur says, he may give us more trouble yet."

ASLO by **MARION PITMAN**

Music in the Bone [Alchemy Press 2016]

What others have said:

It's quite a varied collection of Marion Pitman's work from a number of different sources and spans a long career of writing. Within this collection we have twenty pieces; some very short, almost motifs and some poetry, but all clearly expressed... Music in the Bone *is a lovely collection of diversions and adds a new tome to the Alchemy Press shelf of intelligent, adult, urban fantasy. There are messages to find here; characters to like, love and hate; places to remember and ideas to stir the mind.* — SF Book website

(Marion Pitman's) stories are about people who discover that the floorboards of reality are much thinner than they had supposed, and in some cases have been removed altogether. – John Dallman

Music in the Bone is available from Amazon, The Book Depository and other online dealers. Also available for your Kindle.

ABOUT THE WRITERS

 **Donald Yule** is a retired Charity Finance Director, whose first venture into published fiction this is, after publishing a long-awaited Family Memoir in 2019. Now a resident of St Leonard's on Sea, East Sussex, Donald was a familiar figure for many years in the stand at Rosslyn Park FC and supporting Middlesex CCC from the Pavilion at Lord's Cricket Ground, as rugby and cricket have been lifetime interests and he has performed many roles in both sports. Having earlier contributed to those games in Warrington and Widnes, he will also be remembered in Merseyside and London as a formidable player of the intense Mind Sport, Team Quizzing. Retired also from that activity and honoured with the Life Presidency of the Quiz League of London which he founded, Donald finds time to support his local club, Hastings & Bexhill RFC and still likes short walks and long lunches.

Marion Pitman is a Londoner by heritage and inclination whose fiction and poetry has been published regularly since 1979. Her first short-story collection, *Music in the Bone,* came out from Alchemy Press in 2016, and her work has appeared in a number of anthologies and  magazines. She mostly writes ghost stories, but also dabbles in science fiction, fantasy and westerns. She is also a lifelong cricket enthusiast and Middlesex supporter.

ALSO BY DONALD YULE

on the www.CompletelyNovel.com platform

OTHER TIMES, OTHER PLACES is a book based on the unique diaries kept by two unremarkable, young Scots at two different times on two different sojourns in two different continents in the 1930's. The two Scots are the author's Mum and Dad whose observations of travel to and life in Western Australia and then Sierra Leone give a fascinating glimpse of a vanished era. The modern reader is given a picture of the background of both Diarists in industrial central Scotland and of the society which shaped their attitudes to the pioneering culture where they found themselves. Acclaimed for its comprehensive research and explanatory notes, the book includes hitherto unpublished sketches and rarely seen photographs and the cooperation of Family and Industrial Historians has enabled the inclusion of current illustrations of those scenes.

250 pp softback ISBN 978-1-787823-285-3
Obtainable directly from:
www.CompletelyNovel.com/books/other-times-other-places
or via Amazon and other online sources.

Royalties from the sales of this book are forwarded in full to the Royal National Lifeboat Institution

www.ingramcontent.com/pod-product-compliance
Lightning Source LLC
Chambersburg PA
CBHW071538100726
47908CB00004B/1427